THE UP-DOWN

Portrait of Pace Ripley by Barry Gifford

THE
UP-DOWN

The almost lost, last
Sailor and Lula story,
in which their son,
Pace Roscoe Ripley,
finds his way

BARRY GIFFORD

Seven Stories Press
NEW YORK

This book is for Tita Sorcia—
"en las estrellas que hay
sobre el firmamento del Veracruz"

Excerpts from *The Up-Down* have appeared in the magazines *Nexos* (Mexico City), *Hotel Amerika* (Chicago), *Vice* (New York), and, in different form, *The Chicagoist* (Chicago).

Seven Stories Press
140 Watts Street
New York, NY 10013
sevenstories.com

Cover painting "Woman with Mountain Lion" by Holly Roberts, 1985. The drawing of Pace Ripley is by Barry Gifford. The anecdote on page 188 involving Aurelio Audaz and the old Mascogo is credited by the author in part to Guillermo Arriaga and in homage to Jorge Luis Borges.

Library of Congress Cataloging-in-Publication Data

Gifford, Barry, 1946-
  The up-down / Barry Gifford. -- First edition.
    pages cm
  ISBN 978-1-60980-577-7 (hardback)
  1. Young men--Fiction. I. Title.
PS3557.I283U73 2015
813'.54--dc23
                                      2014004825

Printed in the USA

9 8 7 6 5 4 3 2 1

"Death is nothing, nor life either,
for that matter."
—MATA HARI

". . . if I turn mine eyes upon myself,
I find myself a traitor with the rest."
—WILLIAM SHAKESPEARE

Part One

Following the death of his mother, Lula Pace Fortune Ripley, Pace Roscoe Ripley, who was at that time living in New Orleans, was seized by a desire to turn his life in a new direction. Pace was fifty-eight years old and he had been engaged in the rebuilding of his home place of N.O. after the devastating damage done to that city due to the flood caused by the failure of the levees occasioned by Hurricane Katrina. Now that both his parents had passed, and with no really significant sentimental attachment to keep him there, Pace resolved to find a solution more personal and closer to his heart. He completed the renovation projects already underway, then dissolved his small construction company, said goodbye to those who had worked with and for him, and, without fanfare, left town.

During the several weeks it took him to complete his affairs in N.O., Pace spent a considerable amount of time deliberating about which direction to go. Years before, he had read that in ancient times various societies, including the Irish, Chinese and Indo-European cultures, believed there were five directions: North, South, East, West and the Up-Down, which represented the navel or center. He had remembered this ever since he'd learned of it, and liked the idea of a fifth, mysterious direction. The center of things is where Pace decided to go. Having lived for periods in places as diverse as New York City and Kathmandu, Nepal, he knew that geography had nothing to do with it, that the signs of the Up-Down pointed inward, that it was time for him to figure out exactly what that meant, and that to get there he had to travel alone.

2

"I once knew a man whose senses were so acute that he could hear a flea dancing on a silk handkerchief."

Pace studied the face of the man who said this. He had introduced himself as Dr. Boris Furbo, of Lake Geneva, Wisconsin, soon after Pace had sat down next to him on the City of New Orleans, the passenger train running between N.O. and Chicago. Dr. Furbo, who looked to be in his late sixties or early seventies, wore a yellow-and-white-dotted bow tie with a green seersucker suit. He had almost no hair on his head or on his face, including eyebrows, which were mere creases under his forehead. His rimless, blue-tinted eyeglasses were perilously sustained by a nose no larger than the thumb of a seven year old child. He explained to Pace that he was returning to Wisconsin from a conference on hysterogenics, which he defined for Pace as the study of the origins of unsuitable and/or uncontrollable sexual behavior. The doctor claimed that his clinic in Lake Geneva offered the only reliable treatment for this condition, the mandatory textbook being his own *Guide to Furbotics: The Cauterization Theory and Its Uses, Including a Cessation Process Evidenced by the Eradication of Varietal Types of Caterwauling.* Dr. Furbo dug a copy of the book out of a brown boarhide satchel set on the floor between his feet and handed it to Pace.

"Here, my man," said the doctor. "After you've read it,

you'll never think the same way again about Ingrid Munch's Oslo Syndrome."

Dr. Furbo suddenly stood and picked up his satchel. Pace was surprised at how tall he was, perhaps six foot six or seven. Furbo strode to the far end of the car and went through the connecting door to the next. Pace did not see him again for the remainder of his journey to Chicago, which, excepting this brief encounter with the dubious doctor, was uneventful. As to the book, each page was entirely blank except for the word "Fin" on the very last, which Pace knew was French for The End.

3

Pace had saved some money from his construction projects in New Orleans and he had inherited a small amount from his mother upon her death, as well as Dalceda Delahoussaye's house in Bay St. Clement, North Carolina, in which Lula had been living. Pace had contracted with a realty company in Bay St. Clement to rent the house, so he also had a little income from that. He felt a bit guilty for leaving New Orleans, but following Lula's death for some reason he felt unusually restless, as if the spirits of both his parents were summoning him, calling from the Great or Not-So-Great Beyond, wherever or whatever that might be, to hurl himself off the cliff of Been There into the ocean of What Could Be. Other than his former paramour Marnie Kowalski, with whom Pace had remained on appreciably more than good terms, and Luther Byu-Lee, a musician whose house he had rebuilt in the Lower Nine, Pace figured there wasn't anyone in N.O that he would miss spending time with more than the ordinary. He'd never been one for hanging on the telephone and he didn't e-mail, text or tweet. Pace did like to send postcards, however, so as long as there was still a United States Postal Service he could keep in touch with those few individuals still on the prowl in the active file of his cerebral cortex.

He knew nobody in Chicago and very little about the city except that it got extremely cold in the winter and the powerful wind that blew in off of Lake Michigan was called The Hawk. It was June now, so cold would not be an immediate problem; and even if it got hot and sticky the humidity wouldn't have anything on summer in New Orleans. When he disembarked from the train at Union Station, Pace stood for a few minutes on the platform looking around and thinking about what he should do first. There was no sign of Dr. Furbo.

Pace had a backpack and a roller suitcase. All of his other possessions he'd stored in a shed in the yard behind Marnie Kowalski's house on Orleans Street. He walked to the taxi stand and asked a driver to take him to a not-too expensive but clean small hotel near the Art Institute. Pace had always wanted to see the original of Georges Seurat's painting *La Grande Jatte,* which he knew was on permanent display there. This was one thing he'd long desired to do so it seemed like a good start. On the drive over, Pace hummed softly the tune "In a Small Hotel," the way he'd so often listened to it played by the tenor saxophonist Stan Getz.

"You ever been in Chicago before?" the driver asked.

"No," said Pace. "Always wondered about it, though. Heard good things."

"Well, it's a city like any other, only bigger than most. Some good things, as you say, some bad. Where you from?"

"New Orleans."

"I had family in Louisiana," said the driver. "Close by Baton Rouge. They all passed now, though."

"Did you ever get down there?"

"Yes, sir, a few times when I was a boy, but that was more than forty years ago. Recall catchin' catfish with my cousin Charles, with our hands. Charles showed me how to hold 'em without those sharp spears poke out both sides of their head don't cut you up."

"That was good of him. Catfish cuts can be plenty nasty."

"Yes, sir. Poor Charles, though, he only made it to sixteen years old when he got shot bein' in a wrong place at a wrong time, buyin' a RC Cola in a convenience store when some fool tried to rob it. Clerk took up a pistol and kept firin' until all the bullets was used. One of 'em hit Charles in the head. Robber got away."

"That's a sad story," said Pace.

"Mm-hmm. I'll take you to a little hotel two blocks from the art museum, the Blackhawk, named after the Indian chief lived around here back in the day. They call it a boo-teek, 'cause of the size, but it's priced very reasonable and decent folks work there. My sister, Marvis, she works on the reception desk. Tell her Arvis brought you by."

"Arvis and Marvis, huh?"

"Uh huh. Got a brother named Parvis, the oldest. Our mama had a real affection for rhymin'. She told me she'd had a fourth child, she would have named him Jarvis, or if it was a girl, Narvis. Here we are now."

Pace was checked into the Blackhawk by Marvis, who told him that her brother brought customers to the hotel only if he had a good feeling about them. She gave Pace a room on the fourth floor with windows overlooking the street. Pace lay down on the bed and immediately fell asleep. He dreamt that he was a little boy again and he was riding in the back seat of his father's car. Sailor and Lula were in the front. Sailor was driving as night fell. "Daddy," Pace said in his dream, "aren't you gonna turn on the headlights?" Lula turned around and smiled at him. Her face was silvery blue in the dusk light. "Don't worry, darlin'," she said, "we don't need them any more."

4

The first thing Pace did the next day at the Art Institute was look at Seurat's painting. It was much larger than he'd expected it to be and he was pleased to finally be standing in front of it, but he was disappointed that it was covered by glass and at certain angles was difficult to see properly. After he'd had enough of *La Grand Jatte*, Pace toured most of the rest of the museum, then went outside and stood near one of the lion statues at the entrance and watched the traffic crawl by.

He thought about his parents, Sailor and Lula, and how impossible it seemed to him that neither of them was alive. As long as his mother was still on the planet, Pace felt that Sailor, even though he had preceded Lula to the promised land by fifteen years, through her remained near by, his spirit if not his consciousness embodied in Lula. She was forever "consulting" Sailor, as she put it, considering what he would do or say in a certain situation. At least Pace had had a good last visit with his mother when she and her dearest and most enduring friend, Beany Thorn, had driven down from North Carolina to New Orleans to see him. The fact that Beany had been with Lula when she expired consoled Pace some. Anyway, he was almost sixty years old now and he'd led an interesting life, from N.O. to New York, to Nepal, Los Angeles and back to N.O. The problem, Pace had realized for a long time, was that he had been marked so deeply by the mutual devotion of his parents. Their undying love was a kind of miracle, he believed, and the fact that he never found the Big Love he expected to show up made Pace wonder if his own life had been a failure. Perhaps if he and his ex-wife, Rhoda Gombowicz, had had children, he would feel differently. He'd loved Rhoda but their time had run out thirty years ago. She was gone now, too, of course. After they'd divorced and Pace had taken himself off to Kathmandu, Rhoda had gone back to college and become a primate ethnologist. While doing fieldwork in Rwanda, studying gorillas, she was killed by poachers who had in an effort to cover up their crime dismembered her body and buried the parts in different places in the jungle. Only Rhoda's head and her left leg were found and returned by the Rwandan government to her parents.

Pace had read about her death and the circumstances of it by chance in a month-old copy of *The International Herald Tribune* while he was recovering in Bangalore, India, from two broken ankles suffered during a trek in the Himalayas. Rhoda's murder was investigated but the perpetrators had never been found. Harvard University, which had funded her research, apparently mounted a plaque in Rhoda's honor on a wall in their anthropology department but Pace had never gone to Cambridge, Massachusetts, to see it. He had, however, visited Rhoda's grave, which, of course, contained only the remains of her head—one ear was missing—and one leg, in a cemetery at Montauk, Long Island, where her parents, Irving and Greta Gombowicz, had gone to live following Irving's retirement from the New York City Fire Department. Engraved on Rhoda's tombstone, other than her name and dates of birth and death, were the words: "Her Heart Is With The Animals She Loved."

It was time, Pace decided, while watching a red Toyota Prius being driven by a woman talking on a cell phone rear end a city bus, to get serious about the Up-Down.

5

Pace found a one-bedroom apartment on the far north side on Balkanski Avenue just off Clark Street, a few blocks from the town of Evanston, Illinois. It was a third floor walk up with two families of Ukrainian immigrants occupying the floors below. He had very little to do with the immediate neighbors other than to greet them on the stairs; Pace never heard any of the Ukrainians speaking English and they kept to themselves. Pace did also. Though ordinarily gregarious, he needed this time alone, to be virtually anonymous in a city whose population took no heed of him nor had need of him. For the first time in his life, Pace felt like a wandering ghost. Nobody was waiting for him and neither, really, was he expecting anyone to come along and tell him what to do. He had not felt so cut off from the rest of the world since he had been kidnapped at the age of ten in N.O. by a crazy boy named Elmer Désespéré; this was different though, because now he was alone.

When he lived in Kathmandu, Pace had half-assedly studied Buddhist texts, but he was then too preoccupied with worldly things to give them proper attention. Sailor and Lula were not churchgoers except for Lula's short-lived infatuation with the Church of Reason, Redemption and Resistance to God's Detractors, which ended abruptly after the church's corrupt preacher, Reverend Goodin Plenty, was gunned down by an unhinged member of the flock in Rock Hill, South Carolina. This incident took place in front of Lula's eyes and she soon thereafter gave up on organized religion in any form. The assassination of Goodin Plenty occurred during Pace's forced incarceration by Elmer Désespéré, so he had not known much about it at the time, and Pace had no specific religious instruction thereafter. His subsequent readings of various theories regarding ontology failed to impress him, though he considered the Old Testament of the King James Bible to be the granddaddy of all *noir* novels, and the New Testament to be the model for what popularly came to be known as science fiction.

Sailor had his own oddball theory about reincarnation that he called "sprinkle bodies," which Pace thought made about as much sense as anything else. Religion, Pace thought, either made people mean or kind, according to their interpretation of whichever book or teachings laid down the law by which they had decided to abide. He realized, however, that at this crucial point in his life he was in dire need of some kind of guidance, sign or revelation. If it were to come from within, the Up-Down, he had to figure out how to climb on that wave and ride until it or he gave out.

Pace took to taking long walks along the shore of Lake Michigan as well as through the simmering summertime streets. The people he encountered were mostly polite but not particularly outgoing, largely unwilling to engage or be engaged in the sometimes too-often overly friendly and confessional way people are in New Orleans. That was all right with Pace, though; his demands upon and expectations of the human race were rapidly diminishing. His happiest moments came when he sat on his back porch late at night looking out over the alleys and backyards listening to the sounds made by his neighbors in their kitchens, dogs barking and cats whining and wailing. Best of all was when it rained, especially if there was thunder and lightning, which was often spectacular. He loved smelling the rain in the wind and when the rain came Pace could almost forget about the terrible behavior going on all over the world. There had to be a reason to exist, he thought, other than only for the sake of existing. And how did death figure into the equation? Rhoda murdered by ape poachers, Sailor killed in a senseless car wreck, Lula passing at eighty of so-called natural causes. What was natural or unnatural about anyone's demise? Weren't all of them threads in an unfinished fabric? Here he was, most certainly in the final quarter of his earthly residence, sitting on a back porch in the midwest having a dialogue with the night and discovering that he was more curious than ever about the purpose of everything, and wondering why thinking about it made him feel so ridiculous.

6

Pace had kept the book Dr. Furbo had given him on the train, even though the pages were blank. Perhaps there was a point to the lack of content other than the French word for End. Pace removed the *Guide to Furbotics* from his suitcase and re-read the subtitle. Perhaps this bizarre creature Dr. Furbo meant to signify that people should just quit complaining; "the eradication of caterwauling" could be interpreted that way. Where was it that Furbo claimed to have established his clinic? Lake Geneva, Wisconsin, Pace remembered. He decided to call information in Lake Geneva to find out if there really was such an institution.

"Hello, operator, do you have a listing in Lake Geneva for a Dr. Furbo, or a medical clinic, health farm or spa with that name? You do? Furbo Reinclination and Redefinition Projects. That must be it. Is there an address? Yes, please. Thank you." Pace wrote down the telephone number and address the operator gave him. Perhaps Dr. Furbo wasn't just a nut. Pace decided to go to Lake Geneva and find out.

Pace rented a car and drove from Chicago into Wisconsin, a state he had never entered before. Unfortunately, whenever he thought about Wisconsin, he recalled reading about the gruesome murders committed by a farmer named Ed Gein, back in the early 1960's; and, more recently, the equally ghastly killings conducted in Milwaukee by Jeffrey Dahmer.

Both men had apparently been guilty of cannibalism; and, in Gein's case, using human skin to make lampshades, as the Nazis had done after flaying the corpses of Jews and Gypsies. The other things Pace associated with Wisconsin were beer and cheese.

Lake Geneva was a resort town: swimming and hiking in summer, skiing in winter. Pace drove to the center of town and stopped into a convenience store where he bought a bottle of root beer—they didn't carry Barq's, so he settled for Dad's—and asked the clerk at the register for the best route to Warren Spahn Road. The clerk, who, Pace guessed, was in his late teens or very early twenties, told him to head east four and a half miles and he'd run into it.

"Do you know who Warren Spahn was?" Pace asked the clerk.

"No, sir."

"The winningest left-handed pitcher in major league history. Won three hundred sixty three games. Pitched mostly for the Milwaukee Braves in the 1950's and '60s. He's in the Hall of Fame."

"He must be an old man now."

"He's dead."

Pace gave the boy a dollar and told him to keep the change.

"Sorry, sir," said the clerk, "but the root beer's a dollar and a half."

Pace dug another dollar out of one of his pockets, put it down on the counter, said, "Forgot I'm up north," and walked out of the store.

He found Warren Spahn Road and bent right, the only direction he could go. There were no houses on either side of the road, only birch trees, which Pace found quite beautiful. He thought about Spahn pitching against Juan Marichal in a famous game in which they each posted goose eggs until Willie Mays homered for the Giants in the bottom of the sixteenth inning to beat the Braves. Both pitchers used a high leg kick when they wound up to disguise the ball and throw off the hitter's timing. Pace could not think of a single pitcher in the major leagues who employed that technique in the present day.

The deeper Pace drove into the woods the darker it got. The sun was going down fast and Pace sped up. After several miles, he turned on the headlights. Just as the final sliver of daylight slipped away, Pace saw a sign at the entrance to a gravel driveway on the driver's side of the road. Hand-lettered in black on a white board were the words: DR. BORIS FURBO, SCIENTIST-PHILOSOPHER-ENGINEER OF HUMAN SOLACE, ENTER HERE BUT KEEP IN MIND THAT THERE IS ALWAYS A TRADE OFF.

Pace turned in and headed up the driveway. Lights were on in a two-story house. Parked in front of the house was a 1955 black Cadillac hearse. Pace pulled up next to it, cut his engine, got out of the car and slowly walked toward the house.

7

"By virtue of the fact that you sought me out and have understood the purpose of my book, if not the precise meaning, I invite you to remain and study with me. All intelligent seekers sooner or later realize that a teacher is necessary to their development. The most important part of knowing is knowing when you will never know. No and Know are non-exclusive antitheses of both Virtual and Repugnant Paradox. Even Einstein and, later, the unfortunate Gödel, decided that there was indeed a Desirable Gap. The question this provokes, of course, is how to process regret without falling prey to the Jonah Compulsion, which Gödel called Informal Fallacy, or some such nonsense. Are you hungry?"

Pace had been listening to Dr. Furbo for two hours. What Furbo had to say about knowing and not knowing reminded Pace of something but he could not remember exactly what.

"Yes, Dr. Furbo. I'm both hungry and a little tired."

Furbo jumped up from the large wicker rocking chair in which he had been sitting.

"I'll barbecue some spare ribs, then," he said. "I'm in the fourth week of the Bromige-Rosen Diet. First week, potatoes and oatmeal; second week, collard greens and dandelion soup; third week, pasta and ice cream; fourth week, ribs and beer. Bromige-Rosen recommend beer be taken only twice a day, but since there are to be four feedings per day, I find it a tad difficult not to imbibe with each serving. I'm looking forward to next week's menu of sauerkraut and honeydew melon. No fish in Bromige-Rosen; absolutely *verboten*. I agree entirely. All fish carry the undetectable funambular cell, which causes vertigo."

"If the cell is undetectable," Pace said, "how do you know fish carry it?"

"Molecular deviation detected centuries ago by the Mesopotamians. They were the pioneers of ichthyology, did all their work in the Tigris and Euphrates rivers. Everyone credits the Egyptians but they were just the first to alter their diet by decree. No pharaoh ever expired due to funambular seizure, remember that."

Pace fell asleep in Dr. Furbo's attic guest room following his having heartily partaken of a slab of beef ribs slathered with the doctor's original sauce, which recipe included a modest dash of Chiefland, Florida, boar urine.

"That's what gives it such a lively undertaste," Furbo informed Pace.

Late the next morning Pace awoke feeling slightly sick to his stomach and thought immediately of the boar urine in the barbecue sauce. He dressed and went downstairs and found Dr. Furbo, all seventy-nine inches of him, still dressed as he had been the night before in a black suit with a black shirt and black tie, stretched out on the kitchen floor with his eyes closed and not moving.

"Dr. Furbo, are you all right?" Pace shouted into the doctor's right ear.

Furbo did not budge. Pace knelt down and felt the doctor's left hand. The fingers were cold and slightly stiff. His chest was not rising and falling. Pace stood up and looked at Furbo. He had not noticed until now a deep indentation on the far right side of Furbo's forehead. Pace used a wall telephone in the kitchen to dial O.

"Hello, operator, could you please connect me to the police? I want to report a death."

While he waited for the police to arrive, Pace took a look around the livingroom. An open book lay on the coffee table. It was *The Confidence Man* by Herman Melville. At the top of page 88, underlined in red pencil, was the title of Chapter 17: "Towards the End of Which The Herb-Doctor Proves Himself a Forgiver of Injuries."

8

As Pace pulled out of Dr. Furbo's driveway, it began to rain. He recalled the final sentence of Faulkner's novel, *Sanctuary*, or part of it: "it was the season of rain and death." Dr. Furbo's sudden demise seemed to Pace a terrible portent of things to come, as if wherever he went death would insist on his keeping company. The rain increased. Pace could not remember ever having such a convincing feeling of foreboding. The most important part of knowing, Dr. Furbo instructed, is knowing when you'll never know. Sailor would have probably called Dr. Furbo a crank or a kook, Pace thought, but not Lula. His mother kept more of an open mind and would study on the vagaries of No and Know.

Another thing the deceased doctor said was that the term simple-minded had acquired an undeservedly onerous definition. When asked how he had been able to endure torture at the hands of the Turks, Dr. Furbo recounted, T.E. Lawrence had replied that the trick is simply to not mind.

Pace had overheard one of the attendants loading Dr. Furbo's body into an ambulance say to another attendant, "This guy used to teach biology at Tecumseh High. My sister, Estelle, was in his class when he got fired for telling them that the only way mankind could avoid extinction was if everyone was inoculated with a partial solution of Javanese violet viper venom and wild boar sperm." For a moment Pace considered telling them about Dr. Furbo's barbecue sauce recipe but he let it go.

If this was indeed the season of rain and death, Pace decided, turning up the windshield wiper speed a notch, he would keep searching for an explanation until the very end. As the men pushed the stretcher bearing Furbo's corpse into the rear of the ambulance, Pace had noticed a small syringe sticking out from the doctor's right ankle. What had he injected into himself, Pace wondered, knowing he would never know. Suddenly, Pace realized that he did not mind.

9

Pace decided to leave Chicago, but before he did he went back to the Art Institute to see once more Seurat's great painting. He paid particular attention to the monkey in the foreground, and was reminded of something else Dr. Furbo said: If animals have the ability to reason, which they do, why is it that they do not believe in God?

Pace bought a 2003 midnight blue Ford F-150 truck and headed southwest. Twenty years before, when he had lived in Los Angeles and worked as an assistant to various film producers and directors, he'd always meant to take a vacation and explore the other western states but had never found the time. Now there was nothing to prevent him from doing so. Pace felt good driving so he kept at it, stopping only for gas and food and at cheap motels to sleep. He was not in need of conversation, so he kept exchanges with people to a polite minimum. His brief but intense encounter with Dr. Furbo had convinced Pace that the only path to the Up-Down would be of his own devising. Despite Furbo's oddball theories and strange antics, there was no doubt in Pace's mind that the man had been sincere in his quest for the answers to the fundamental questions that had puzzled and virtually stupefied man since the Big Three, as the doctor called them, had first sizzled in a human being's brain pan, those being What? How? and Why?

One morning in Gila Bend, Arizona, Pace woke up and remembered his dream of the night before. In the dream several women were sitting in a room around a table. Three or four of the women were smoking cigarettes, one of whom Pace recognized to be Lula as she was in her twenties. In the room, which was dimly lit by small lamps with red shades, was a dark shape that moved around as the women talked. The women seemed not to notice this dark shape, or at least paid it no attention. Pace could not understand what the women were saying but they all seemed quite contented and calm. One of the women stood up and was immediately absorbed by the dark shape, but the others went on with their conversation. When Pace awakened he realized that the woman who had disappeared was his mother.

The desert was too hot so Pace headed north. His destination was Wyoming, a state he had never visited but whose name had a mythical quality for him. As a child, Pace and Lula had used Wyoming as an imaginary idyll, a place where nothing bad could happen, a kind of magical land. His mother had never been in Wyoming, either; nor, to Pace's knowledge, had Sailor. Whenever Lula made up a story to tell Pace at bedtime she would end it by saying, "and they all lived happily ever after in Wyoming." He no longer believed this, of course, but the closer he got to Wyoming, the cooler the air became.

Once he was in Wyoming, Pace avoided cities, such as Laramie, and tourist meccas like Jackson Hole. He wound his way along two-lane roads and stopped in a mountain town malignantly named, old Hollywood western-style, Dead Indian. Pace parked his pick-up in front of a bar called Frank's X, and went inside.

It was four o'clock in the afternoon. Two men wearing brown Stetsons were seated on stools at the bar and four men wearing brown Stetsons sat singly at four tables. There was one bartender, hatless, with a long ponytail and Fu Man Chu mustache, wearing a gray T-shirt with the words TRY AGAIN LATER printed on the front of it. Pace sat down on a stool at the bar. Above the shelves of bottles opposite him was a large, framed black and white photograph of a nude woman lying on a white fur-covered couch with a black dog, its tongue hanging out, sitting up near her feet, staring at the camera.

"Go ahead, ask me," the bartender said to Pace. "Everybody comes in here the first time does."

"Who is she?" Pace asked.

"Frank's ex-wife."

"Frank own this bar?"

"Used to. After the divorce, she shot and killed him."

"Why after the divorce?"

"Everything Frank had he put in his mother's name before so Malaysia couldn't take it."

"What happened to Malaysia?"

"Split after she shot Frank. Word is she's in Cambodia, married to a general in the Cambodian army. Cambodia don't have an extradition treaty with the United States. Don't expect Malaysia coming back any time soon, especially to Dead Indian. What'll it be?"

"Beer. Anything Mexican, if you have it."

The bartender put a bottle of Negra Modelo on the bar, opened it and placed a glass next to it. Pace laid down a five dollar bill. The bartender picked it up and turned around to work the cash register. Written on the back of his T-shirt were the words ON SECOND THOUGHT, DON'T.

The bartender turned back around and put down three singles. One of the Stetsons who'd been sitting at a table went over to the jukebox and dropped in a few coins, all of which clattered into the change receptacle. Skeeter Davis began singing "Am I That Easy To Forget?"

"I haven't seen an old Rock-ola like that for a while," Pace said.

"Frank's. He rigged it so it don't cost anything to play the records. Just gotta put in the silver, take it back. All the 45s were Frank's, too. Most pretty wore out now."

"Frank's mother owns the bar, I assume."

"That's what sent Malaysia over the top. She figured on gettin' the place and when she found out Frank's mother owned it, Malaysia grabbed his Colt Python and ended any debate before it could begin."

Pace drank his Negra Modelo straight from the bottle.

"You lookin' to buy property? Plenty available."

"No, I'm just passin' through."

"We don't get many passers through, Dead Indian bein' somewhere off the beaten track."

"I'm surprised the politically correct committee haven't tried to make you change the town's name. Or have they?"

"This is Wyoming, mister."

"I've heard that line before, in a movie, only with a different name. By the way, mine's Pace Ripley."

"Big Douglas."

They shook hands.

"Big?"

"Yeah. My brother and I are fraternal twins. I'm the bigger one."

"Don't tell me your brother's called Little."

Big grinned. "Shorty," he said.

Pace smiled and nodded.

"What was the movie?" asked Big. "The one with the different name?"

"This is Ames, mister," said Pace. "*The Hustler*, with Paul Newman as Fast Eddie Felson. Only straight pool played there."

"Only sight worth stoppin' to see around here is an unusual rock formation on the side of a mountain looks like two arrows pointin' in opposite directions. Most people call it Two Way but the Shoshone name for it is the Up-Down."

"How do I get there?" asked Pace.

Big told him and Pace left without touching the three singles on the bar.

It took him almost an hour on a rock-strewn, unpaved road

to get to the Up-Down. As soon as he saw it, Pace stopped, got out of the truck and hiked along a narrow path to the edge of the mountain in order to view the formation more closely. On the side was a tall rock shaped like an arrow on the top that pointed to the sky; appended to it was another rock, also with an arrow-shaped formation at the tip, pointing down. On the right-side ledge of the south pointing arrow was an eagle's nest in which Pace could see the downy heads of two baby bald eagles. He'd never before seen eagles in the wild, so he lay flat and hung over the precipice as far as he could to take a better look.

Just then Pace heard a loud noise that sounded like "frap, frap," followed by an eardrum-piercing screech. He turned and saw an enormous bald eagle, its talons extended and poised to rip into his flesh, descending upon him. As Pace fell, he remembered what it was that he could not at Dr. Furbo's. In Jack London's novel, *Martin Eden*, when Martin is drowning, London wrote, "At the instant he knew, he ceased to know." Before hitting the ground, Pace knew he had reached the very end and that there would be no explanation for anything.

Part Two

1

Pace did not die. After he fell from the ledge, he suffered a severe head injury on impact with the outcropping below, on which he landed and broke both legs. He was found, unconscious, by a pair of hikers, a man and a woman, whose names he never learned and whom he never met. They managed to get him to a hospital and departed. All he was able to learn later, from a nurse who attended him in the emergency room, was that the couple was apparently from Iceland and that the man bore a startling resemblance to the actor Robert Ryan.

Pace eventually made his way to Bay St. Clement, North Carolina, where he took up residence in a cottage on Dalceda Delahoussaye's property, which, of course, he had in turn inherited from his mother, Lula. The main house was rented to a young couple, a high school history teacher and his wife, who worked as a landscape architect. For several weeks after Pace arrived, he was burdened by casts on both legs and was frequently bothered by dizzy spells most likely caused by a concussion. The young woman was of great help to Pace during this period of his recovery, making sure that his basic needs were met, that he ate properly and was as comfortable as possible.

Pace slept often in these weeks and had difficulty determining the difference between dream and reality. After two months, when his mental faculties had returned nearly to normal and he had come to a full understanding of what happened to him, Pace realized that he was most satisfied while in a dream state, abetted as that was by extensive use of pain-killers and barbiturates, from which the doctor who treated him was at this point in Pace's recovery attempting to wean him. Dr. Dacoit had been Dalceda Delahoussaye's physician for the last twenty-two years of her life and had also tended to Pace's mother upon occasion. Though now almost eighty-five years old, Dr. Dacoit was still in possession of his faculties and was the only doctor remaining in Bay St. Clement who made house calls.

"I been meanin' to ask you," Pace said to the doctor one afternoon when he was checking in on Pace's progress, "where your name comes from. I never ran into it before."

"Dacoit is actually a Hindu name, son," said the doctor. "My grandfather, Kapoor, was born in Calcutta and was taken to America before the age of two by an uncle and aunt, who established a dry goods business in Baltimore. Kapoor's father, my great-grandfather, was apparently a member of a murderous gang of thieves. He was himself killed and his wife abducted by a rival band of criminals. She was supposedly sold into sexual slavery and ended up in a cage on the docks of Bombay. Kapoor was taken in by one of her brothers and his wife. The name Dacoit came to be associated with the outlaw band in India and Burma. There are many people who believe this gang is still in operation in the present day, much as the mafia in Sicily and America continue their underworld activities unabated. The word 'dacoity' is commonly used in India to describe a robbery."

"That's very interesting, doctor. You ever consider changing it?"

Dr. Dacoit laughed. He had black smudges under both eyes, a large, hawk-like nose, and a full head of wiry white hair. Though an octogenarian, he did not wear eyeglasses either for reading or distance.

"No, why should I have?" he said. "The word dacoit means nothing in this country, and I've never gone to India or Burma. I would like to have but I never got around to it and now I am too old to travel that far and to deal with the everyday difficulties of life in such a confusing place."

"When can I get these casts off?"

"Next week, I think, Mr. Ripley. How frequent are your headaches now?"

"I usually get them in the late afternoon, but they aren't as bad as before."

"Good, good. I'll renew your prescription for the headaches, but I believe we'll see if you can sleep comfortably without the barbiturates. If you have any problems with that, of course, call me."

"Okay, Dr. Dacoit, I will."

"See you in a week, then."

"Oh, doctor?"

"Yes?"

"What's your first name?"

"Hoyt. Named after a knuckleball pitcher on the Baltimore Orioles."

"Just curious. Thanks."

After Dr. Dacoit left, Pace thought about the randomness of events, how strange that this good and dedicated doctor bore the name of an organization of murderous thugs from another continent. Not very much made sense to Pace these days. His head began to spin and he closed his eyes and tried to sleep. He could not control his dreams any better than he could control the circumstances of his waking life, but he had no desire to try to manipulate his dreams. At least in them, he believed, the unpredictability could do him no harm.

2

Pace recalled the title of the chapter in Herman Melville's *The Confidence Man* he had read prior to leaving Dr. Furbo's house in Wisconsin: "Towards the End of Which the Herb-Doctor Proves Himself a Forgiver of Injuries." It was up to Pace to forgive himself for his foolishness in Shoshone country that resulted in his near fatal accident. Once he regained the use of his legs he began taking hikes in the nearby woods. The section he liked best was down near a tributary of the Cottonmouth River. Unfortunately, these woods were heavily tick-infested and home to a variety of vipers, several of which were venomous. Having grown up in New Orleans, Pace was largely ignorant of the geography of North Carolina. As a boy he had visited the Delahoussayes a couple or three times with Lula, usually on those occasions when staying with his grandmother, Marietta, but he had never really explored the surrounding territory. His father, Sailor Ripley, a native of North Carolina, once he had established himself in N.O., never expressed the slightest interest thereafter in returning to the state in which he had been raised and for one year imprisoned for manslaughter. Sailor had later done time in Texas, too, for armed robbery, causing him to miss several of Pace's formative years, and had no desire to ever revisit the Lone Star state, either. The remainder of his lifetime had been incarceration-free, and he and Lula enjoyed what most people who knew them considered a marriage of mutual devotion, certainly the closest thing to true love Pace had ever witnessed.

Pace had once read in a book about a group of hired guns who operated on the plains of northeastern Brazil in the 1920s and '30s, mainly in the states of Mina Gerais and Bahía, whose affiliations with the various landowners for whom they worked lasted until they felt they had "lost their understanding." When this circumstance became unavoidably evident and bothersome to them, this bunch of *jagunços* would announce their condition to the boss and state their intention to move on and find another situation. It never had to do with money, only with their degree of comfort. They made no attempt to further explain their feelings; once their "understanding" was "lost," the resulting action was not subject to debate. The men were mercenaries who always did their best for whomever hired them, their work was never faulted and their loyalty during their period of employment could not be questioned. When it was time to go, they went, without argument.

To be without argument was the way Pace desired to live out the rest of his life. He had no intention of remarrying; his occasional spells of loneliness were more than compensated for by a general sense of tranquility. Pace decided during his first days and weeks of confinement to write about his parents; Sailor and Lula were truly the most interesting people he had ever met. To be wild at heart and never waver on the road to one's destiny was how everyone should live their life. Sailor and Lula had done that, despite several serious tests along the way. Yes, this is what Pace would do, not just as a tribute to his parents but as an inspiration for everyone else struggling along the road to salvation.

Pace dug out from his disorganized pile of belongings Dr. Furbo's book. He would write about Sailor and Lula on the empty pages of Furbo's *Guide*; an appropriate context, Pace thought. Perhaps it might even have been Dr. Furbo's intention for those in possession of a copy to fill in the blanks. He opened the book and wrote the first sentence: "Sailor and Lula lay on the bed in the Cape Fear Hotel listening to the ceiling fan creak."

Part Three

1

Pace found that the writing life agreed with him. He rose each morning at six and began working on his book after he'd had coffee, bread and fruit, usually by seven. He enjoyed imagining what Sailor and Lula's early life together was like. The main theme, Pace decided, was his parents' devotion to one another, what could be considered an intuitive spiritual connection. Lula had told Pace many times that she knew Sailor was destined to be her partner for life from the moment she met him, and that she believed Sailor felt the same way about her. "In these modern times," Pace recalled his mother telling him, "this ain't so usual." Pace was ten years old the first time Lula had said this, the night before his daddy was released from prison after having served a decade behind bars for armed robbery during which two men had been shot and killed, one of them Sailor's accomplice, a person named Bobby Peru, whom Lula referred to as a "black angel." Sailor had not spoken much to Pace about this period of his incarceration, saying only that the penitentiary where he'd done his time, at Huntsville, Texas, was filled with liars, every inmate claiming to be innocent in one way or another of the crime for which he had been convicted. Pace, who was fifteen at the time, had asked Sailor, "Were you innocent, Daddy?" and Sailor answered, "No, son, I was both guilty and a liar. Don't ever blame your troubles on anyone but yourself, and don't be afraid or ashamed to ask for help when you really need it. There'll come a day you will."

2

Bitsy and Delbert Parker, the couple who lived in Dalceda Delahoussaye's big house, were decent, intelligent people. Pace became good friends with them and they often invited him for supper. Del taught at Robert Pete Williams High School, named after the self-styled African-American revolutionary who'd written the book *Negroes with Guns*, and who'd fled the country after committing a crime, then lived most of his life in Red China, as it was then commonly called. The school had originally been named Dogger Bank High, after the site of a naval battle that had been fought in the North Sea during World War I. Times were changing, Del Parker told Pace, even in a state as backward as North Carolina.

Both Del and Bitsy were thirty-two years old. Being childless, and with Del having summers off, they had travelled extensively throughout the world and shared stories of their adventures with Pace, who in turn told them about his own colorful life. Pace felt fortunate to have them as tenants and neighbors.

One cloudy Wednesday afternoon, just as Pace was finishing up his writing for the day, Bitsy knocked on his screen door, which he opened as soon as he saw her.

"I hope I'm not disturbing you," she said.

"No," said Pace, "I'm about done for now. I'm just comin' to the part where Lula tells her mama, Marietta, that she's pregnant with me."

Bitsy laughed, and said, "Well, then, this might could be the right time to talk to you about what I've come to talk to you about."

"Come in. You thirsty?"

Bitsy shook her head no, and they both sat down on a couch in the cottage's front room. Bitsy was a petite, pretty blonde with green eyes. She did a considerable amount of physical work as a landscaper, so she was strong and sinewy with a good figure which Pace could not help but admire. He liked to look at her.

"You may have wondered," she said, "why Del and I have never had children."

"I just figured you hadn't gotten around to it yet."

"Not exactly. The thing is, Del can't shoot nothin' but blanks. I'm okay, though. We had tests to find out why I've never gotten pregnant."

"Rhoda and I never had kids. Now that I'm older, I wish we had. Anyway, you can adopt."

Bitsy shook her head and her honey blonde hair covered the left half of her face. She stared down at the floor for a minute, then looked back at Pace. There was an expression on her face that he had never seen before, a serious, dark look that made him uncomfortable.

"I got somethin' tough to ask you, Pace, and if you think it's crazy, just say so, all right?"

"Go on and ask."

"Would you consider makin' love with me and see if I could get pregnant? I mean, you're Del's and my good friend and landlord, and livin' here together like we do, it just made sense to me when I thought of it."

Pace just stared at Bitsy for a while before he spoke.

"Is this something you and Del decided? I mean, to suggest the idea to me?"

"Not really," said Bitsy.

"This is only your idea, then," Pace said.

Bitsy nodded. "Do you think I'm crazy, Pace? Does the idea appeal to you at all? Do you think I'm attractive?"

"Of course I think you're attractive, Bitsy, but that's hardly the point. If you and Del decided that you wanted my sperm to use *in vitro*, I guess I'd go along with you, but . . ."

"No," she said. "I don't want some test tube full of jizz injected into me. I need to have it done right, the way nature intended."

"Bitsy, I don't know. Anyhow, you'd have to discuss this with Del. He's your husband."

Bitsy slid over next to Pace and kissed him. She put her hand between his legs and fondled him. Pace kissed her back.

She took her mouth off of his and whispered, "It'll work, Pace, I just know it. This is your chance, too. Maybe the last one."

Bitsy stood, took Pace by his left hand with her right, pulled him up, and led him into the bedroom.

3

Pace carried on with Bitsy for a couple of months, rendezvousing with her three or four weekday afternoons while Del was teaching at the high school. This turn of events disturbed him because Del knew nothing of his liaison with Bitsy. Pace asked her what she intended to say to her husband if and when she became pregnant; after all, Pace said, Del had been tested and told he could not father a child. "I'll just tell him it's a miracle," Bitsy answered. "It's proof that miracles do happen, and that he should be happy."

Pace wasn't so sure about Del buying Bitsy's story. What Pace was certain about was that she continued to have sex with Del while she kept on with him. What was happening, Pace realized, was that he was becoming more emotionally involved with Bitsy than she was with him. Bitsy treated their lovemaking sessions with a demeanor Pace found a little too breezy for his taste. Not that she was distant or not tender during their "sessions," as Bitsy called them, it was just that after a while, once he'd gotten over the initial thrill of making love regularly again with a beautiful young woman, Pace began to resent his being used. It would have been better, he decided, to have just donated his sperm and let a doctor inseminate Bitsy with a needle. Pace had fallen a little in love with Bitsy, and he was not happy about it, not under these circumstances.

When Pace confronted her with his feelings, Bitsy looked into his eyes and said, "I been tryin' to suppress my feelings for you, Pace. I was in love with you, I guess, even before we started up. Now I've got a confession to make: Del never has had any medical tests to determine the motility of his sperm. Only I've been examined and the doctor said there's nothing wrong with me, that I should be able to conceive."

"Why didn't Del have a test?" Pace asked.

"I never insisted on it. He's just always said if it happens, it happens. If it doesn't that's okay with him, too. He just says bein' with me is the most important thing."

Bitsy began to cry, and said, "I'm sorry I lied to you, Pace, I truly am now. I suppose you won't want me any more."

Pace didn't say anything for a minute. He wanted to tell Bitsy that despite this revelation he wanted her almost more than ever, but he held his tongue.

"Let me think on it, Bitsy," he said, finally. "Let's both of us take some time to decide what to do."

Bitsy kissed Pace on the cheek and walked out of his cottage. Pace wished right then that Sailor were still alive and that he could ask him what to do. "Leave her be" were the words that popped into Pace's head.

"Thanks, Daddy," he said.

4

Pace left before dawn two mornings following his last conversation with Bitsy. He headed his Pathfinder north with New York City as his intended destination. He left a note tacked to the front door of the big house addressed to both Bitsy and Del, informing them of his sudden desire to revisit New York. He wasn't sure when he'd be back, he'd let them know. Pace took his notebooks with him, planning to continue writing his book about his parents wherever he landed. That was the great thing about being a writer, Pace thought: you could do it anywhere.

If somehow Bitsy had conceived a child fathered by him, Pace did not really want to know. She would certainly tell Del that it was his and they would both be happy. It didn't matter what Pace felt or thought. He welcomed, even depended on his insignificance in the matter. In the end—or the interim, whatever the case might be—one's understanding of one's actions does little or nothing to alter the result. Pace wondered if he had read this somewhere, or was it a product of his own consideration of the circumstances? Perhaps Bitsy was not pregnant—but Pace's intuition told him that she was. What if he were not Bitsy's only lover? That was always a possibility. Time to go. He was no longer needed or particularly wanted, and he had work to do.

Pace suddenly remembered one night about ten o'clock

when he and Bitsy had been walking together on the path between the cottage and the big house, in which Del was correcting his student's exams. She turned her head to say something to Pace when he took her right arm firmly with his left hand and said, "stop." Bitsy had been about to take a step when she looked down and saw a very long water moccasin crawling across the spot on the path where she would have put down her left foot had Pace not held her back. "What a terrible snake," she said, as they watched its silver and red-diamonded body slither past them. Her foot was still suspended above the ground. "I just saved your life," Pace said. "Don't forget it." She finished her step and they smiled at each other. "Not tonight or ever," said Bitsy.

5

Pace's Pathfinder had 75,000 miles on it. It drove a little rough, like the basic pick-up truck it was, but it was roomy enough so that he could sleep comfortably in it if he needed to. He'd bought it from a friend of his mother's, Álvaro Iturri, a Basque from Bilbao, who had married a young widow from nearby Wrightsville Beach, North Carolina, whom he'd met when she was on a European tour following the death of her husband. He then moved with her to Bay St. Clement and bought into a car dealership. Iturri, who was the same age as Pace and had been a merchant seaman for most of his adult life, admitted to Pace that before buying into this business he had known next to nothing about automobiles.

"That's the great thing about America," Álvaro Iturri told Pace, "everything depends upon trust. In Spain, nobody trusts anyone, not even themselves. This is the theme of *Don Quixote*, of course. In America, doubt exists, certainly, but pessimism is not ingrained in peoples' souls the way it is in Spain and the rest of Europe. The one exception, in my experience, is Italy, where the guiding ingredient is corruption. The Italians make up partially for this in other ways, so they can be most amusing but never less than dangerous.

"Now that I am an American, I can tell you this vehicle I am selling you will run well and for a long time. And since you are an American, you can trust that I am telling you the truth. *Buen viaje.*"

The Pathfinder made it to Philadelphia before it broke down. It was while he was having his SUV repaired that Pace met Siempre Desalmado, and began the third act of his life.

6

Pace had never before been in Philadelphia. He got a room in a hotel off Rittenhouse Square, the Hotel Espíritu, and, since the auto repair shop would need two days to fix his SUV, decided to walk around and explore the city. He was on Race Street, near the Greyhound bus station, when he saw a young woman sitting on a suitcase with her face in her hands, crying. Pace stopped and asked her if she needed help and she lifted her head and looked at him. Despite her distraught condition, the woman had the face of an angel—almost oval, an unmarked, olive complexion, with large, dark brown eyes and long, thin eyebrows. Though tears ran down her face, she smiled at Pace, revealing perfect, brilliantly white teeth. She looked to be anywhere in age from sixteen to twenty-six.

"Who doesn't?" she said. "Do you live in Philadelphia?"

"No, I'm in transit, but temporarily delayed due to car trouble."

"What does 'in transit' mean?"

"I'm between here and there. I'm not sure where 'there' is, but my home of late has been in North Carolina."

"You say funny things: 'in transit,' 'home of late.' You are uncertain."

Pace nodded a little. "I guess so," he said. "And you, are you in need of help?"

"I guess so, too. I took a bus from Phoenix, Arizona, to

here, where a friend of mine said there would be a job for me. I called to the place where she was and was told she had been fired and is gone. Now I'm trying to decide what to do."

"Do you have money?"

She shook her head. "Not very much."

"My name is Pace Ripley. Come on, I'll buy you lunch."

The girl stared at him.

Pace smiled, and said, "I won't hurt you. We're both a little stranded and in need. What's your name?"

"Siempre Desalmado."

"I know siempre means always, but desalmado I don't know."

The girl stood up and wiped her eyes. She was even more beautiful than Pace had thought. Somehow her face was both bright and dark at the same time.

"You must not believe it," she said.

"Believe what?"

"That I am what is my name, desalmado. It means heartless, or cruel. I do not like having this name."

"You should change it then."

"Yes," said Siempre, "perhaps I will. You are how old?"

"Fifty-eight. And you?"

"I will be twenty-two tomorrow."

"Happy birthday, Always. Come on, let's get something to eat."

Later that afternoon Pace took Siempre Desalmado with him to his room at the Hotel Espiritu. He told her that she could have the bed and he would sleep on the floor until she found a place for herself.

"Why do you do this for me, Pace?"

"Because of your beauty."

"Do you always tell the truth?" asked Siempre.

"Not even to myself," said Pace.

7

In the middle of their first night together, Pace, who was not quite asleep, felt Siempre take his hand. She drew him up from the floor to the bed.

"You will be more comfortable with me," she whispered.

"*Sin duda,*" Pace said, as they began to make love for the first time.

In the morning, Siempre and Pace made love again. After showering and dressing they left the hotel and had coffee and croissants at a nearby cafe.

"What do you want to do first?" Pace asked.

"Look for work and a place to live."

"You can stay with me until you find a job."

"How long do you plan to stay in Philadelphia?"

Pace shook his head. "I'm making my plans as I go along. I have no intention of abandoning you to the wolves of the desert."

Siempre Desalmado laughed.

"Where do they live, these wolves?"

"Everywhere. They're always on the prowl, seeking the most vulnerable among us."

"You believe I need to be protected from them?"

Pace sipped his coffee.

"We all do," he said.

"Perhaps I am *una loba del desierto*. A wolf in, how is it said in *ingles, ropa de la oveja.*"

"I've seen you without your clothes."

Siempre laughed.

"*Si*, you have."

"You have beautiful fur."

"Fur? Oh, *si, piel.*"

"But you do have the scent of the wild. Not from your body but from your spirit, your soul. *Su alma.*"

"As I told you, I am not heartless like my name says, but I suppose I am not so easy to tame."

"I have no desire to tame you."

Siempre smiled.

"Not yet," she said.

8

Pace was certainly pleased by his acquaintance with Siempre; it was his view of the world that bothered him. Most days now his observations led him to conclude that the majority of the planet's inhabitants were growing increasingly vulgar and ignorant, even stupid. Pace did not enjoy this feeling and wondered if it had always been this way; perhaps he had been too preoccupied or self-absorbed to notice.

In a dream the night before, he had been bitten by a rattlesnake. He had awakened and gone to the bathroom. After getting back into bed he watched Siempre, who slept soundly. Why this sudden detachment? Pace thought. Or was it sudden? Perhaps this condition had developed incrementally and only now could he recognize it. Pace did not feel confused, only saddened. This weight of sadness, he realized, was the result of disappointment in himself, that he had not accomplished more in his nearly six decades of consciousness; also the deaths of both Sailor and Lula. His parents had been extraordinary people, Pace believed, faithful and generous and blessed with a mutual sense of humor that somehow annealed most of the pain that was part of living. He did not feel himself capable of profound let alone original thought. Pace lay awake a long time before Siempre turned and pressed her warm form against his, then he fell back to sleep.

9

Pace spent his mornings writing about his parents. During this time, Siempre Desalmado hit the streets of Philadelphia looking for work. She usually returned by two or three o'clock in the afternoon, and then she and Pace would have lunch and afterwards make love and take a nap together in their room at the Hotel Espíritu. In the evening they'd go to a movie or, if the weather wasn't too bad, take long walks together. This routine went on for several days until one afternoon Siempre did not return. Pace remained in the hotel room all that day and night. When she had not come back by eight o'clock the next morning, Pace went out to look for her. He walked all over the center of the city, even in the alleys, thinking Siempre might have been mugged or worse, and left for dead, but he could not find her. He returned to the hotel twelve hours later, hungry and tired. Pace was about to collapse on the bed when he realized that Siempre's belongings were gone. He was puzzled and looked around for a note, but there was none. She had left, that was all. The next morning, so did he.

10

Pace did not know what to make of Siempre Desalmado's unexplained disappearance. Not only had she not left him a letter or note but according to the hotel staff her departure had passed unnoticed by those who were on duty during the hours Pace had been out searching for her. To his surprise, befuddled as he was by Siempre's defection, Pace had driven halfway back to North Carolina before he realized in which direction he was headed.

It was the middle of the afternoon when in a matter of a few minutes the sky turned almost entirely dark and it began to rain. Pace switched on the Pathfinder's headlights and windshield wipers. Still, he could barely see beyond the hood of his vehicle. Pace took his hands off the steering wheel and felt himself spinning, revolving slowly at first then more rapidly until he was in a vortex, caught in a whirlwind that precluded his being able to discern exactly what was happening or even to think. There was no light now and Pace felt neither fear nor pain. Suddenly, a thought did come: he had entered the Up-Down.

The next thing he knew he was lying on his back in his bed in the cottage in Bay St. Clement and standing over him, looking into his eyes, was Bitsy Parker.

"Oh, Pace, thank goodness," she said, "I'm so glad you've come back. We did it, darlin', we did it! I'm pregnant."

11

Of course Bitsy had told Del that the child she was expecting was his. As far as she could tell, Bitsy said, her husband had no inkling of her affair with Pace. Bitsy then kissed Pace on the lips and said that she had to run to keep an appointment with a client. They'd catch up on his news later.

Pace lay on his bed still puzzling over how he had gotten there, seemingly safe and sound. Through his bedroom window he could see the Pathfinder parked outside. Had he really momentarily experienced being in the Up-Down, Pace wondered, or had that been an illusion? Perhaps that's what the Up-Down is, he reasoned, an illusion. But how did that explain his blanking out on the trip back from Philadelphia? He was certain he had gone there, that Siempre Desalmado was a real person with whom he'd spent time. After all, Bitsy had welcomed him home. Pace noticed that he was fully dressed, but was he in his right mind?

12

In the middle of his second night back home, Pace awoke when he heard a voice say, "God is a disappointment to everyone." He looked around his bedroom in the cottage but he was alone. The voice had been in his head, a voice he did not recognize. Pace was certain of the words, which he contemplated as he lay in the dark. It was a moonless night, lit only faintly by the stars. Pace closed his eyes, wanting to fall back asleep, hoping to hear the voice again.

13

The following morning, while Pace was sitting at the kitchen table in his cottage having a cup of coffee, he opened a book he had taken with him to Philadelphia intending to read, *The Death Ship* by B. Traven. A piece of paper, stationery from the Hotel Espíritu, folded into the book, fluttered out onto the table. Pace picked it up, unfolded and read what was written on it:

THE BOOK OF EXCUSES

This is The Missing Book of the Old Testament unearthed in the Valley of the Nobles in Egypt by Abdoul Kerim a self-described Wolf of the Desert and believed now to have been written by the same Unknown Author who used Solomon as a shield for the Book of Ecclesiastes but in truth was composed by Solomon's mistress a blackskinned woman known only as Shulamith a shepherdess kidnapped by Solomon and kept apart from all others but eunuchs in his palace in Jerusalem therefore it was she who said There is an evil which I have seen under the sun and it is common among men.

Adios,
Siempre

14

"If it's a boy," Bitsy said, "I'd like to name him Sailor. And if it's a girl, Lula. Only if it's all right with you, of course."

Pace said nothing. He was sitting at his desk and was actually in the middle of writing a sentence when Bitsy entered the cottage without knocking and told him this. Her announcement, Pace realized, was not totally unexpected by him. At least she had not suggested that the child, whether it was male or female, be named Pace.

Bitsy stood next to him, caressing her swollen belly with her right hand. The fingers of her left hand were entwined in her hair, which she had let grow long. Bitsy's honey-colored hair was not only longer now but more lustrous. She had never looked better to Pace but for some reason he fought the feeling.

"Come on, Pace, tell me what you think. Even though I didn't know your parents, I feel like I almost do through you. What you've told me and the way you are. Also, I love their names."

Pace stared at Bitsy, looking her over up and down. Most women, he thought, became more beautiful when they were pregnant, even if they didn't think so, and Bitsy was no exception. Her color was richer due to the twenty-five percent more blood in her body. She glowed. This was not the same woman with whom he had made love.

Finally, Pace said, "Have you asked Del what he thinks?"

Bitsy nodded. "I have. He's happy leavin' the namin' to me."

"It's okay, I guess."

Bitsy pushed herself up against Pace and kissed him on the top of his head.

"Thank you, darlin'," she said. "It'll mean a lot to me, just like you do."

Pace placed his right hand over hers. She put it under her own, on her stomach.

"That's little Lula or Sailor kickin' in there, Pace. Ain't it just thrillin' knowin' that?"

"It's still a little hard to believe."

"Not for me," said Bitsy.

After she left, Pace looked at his interrupted sentence. "Men got a kind of automatic shutoff valve" Lula was telling Sailor. Pace wrote: "in their head? Like, you're talkin' to one and just gettin' to the part where you're gonna say what you really been wantin' to say, and then you say it and you look at him and he ain't even heard it. Not like it's too complicated or somethin', just he ain't about to really listen."

Pace stopped writing and looked out the window in front of his desk. A large crow landed in the yard and stared so hard and fixedly at him that Pace turned away. When he looked again, the crow had gone and a little rain was falling.

15

In the fifth month of Bitsy's pregnancy, her sister, Rapunzelina Cruz, came to stay with Bitsy and Del. Rapunzelina was twelve years younger than Bitsy, the baby of the family. She had been living in Mexico City for the past two and a half years where she'd married a much older man named Abstemio Cruz, a cocktail lounge singer and piano player who specialized in harmlessly crooning the songs of Águstin Lara, Johnny Mathis, Dean Martin and Fred Buscaglioni. Rapunzelina was finished, she told Del and Bitsy, with her husband and Mexico, both of which had lost their charm: the city because of its impossible traffic, smog and all too common physical dangers such as rape, robbery and kidnapping for ransom; and Señor Cruz, who turned out to be an insufferable and abusive drunk. Rapunzelina intended to stay in North Carolina and go back to college, which she had dropped out of after her sophomore year. In Mexico she tried to convince herself she was a painter, having fallen under the spell of the myth of Frida Kahlo, whom she now considered to be vastly overrated as an artist. Rapunzelina admitted to herself that she possessed no real talent and planned to go to nursing school and devote herself to helping people. She had not, however, told her husband that she had no intention of going back to Mexico City or to him and feared that might become a problem if he decided to come after her. When she met Pace and mentioned this, Pace asked, "What are the chances of that?" "We'll see," was all Rapunzelina said.

Rapunzelina did not know when she arrived that it most probably was Pace who was the father of her sister's child. Her predilection for men considerably older than herself had not abated and soon after moving into Dalceda Delahoussaye's house she set about advertising her availability to Pace. Not only was Rapunzelina twelve years younger than Bitsy but she was even more attractive and not shy about wearing skimpy outfits that showcased her hourglass figure and amply complemented her abundant ash-blonde hair and green cat's eyes. She took to visiting Pace in his cottage at late hours and for the first few weeks of her residence he resisted her obvious advances. He feared straining his relations with Bitsy, who gave clear indications to Pace of wanting to resume a sexual component to their friendship. This, too, Pace avoided. He had no exaggerated belief in his own attractiveness and had never thought of himself as an exceptional ladies man, even less so now that he was nearing sixty years old. It was a mystery to him why this was happening.

Then one night Rapunzelina—whom Del and Bitsy and now Pace called Punzy, her childhood nickname—knocked on Pace's door and when he answered asked him, "Is it true, Pace? Are you the one knocked up Bitsy?"

"Did Bitsy tell you that?"

"Who else could have? She spilled the beans after I told her I had a crush on you. Here I've been tryin' to get you to screw me and all the time you're my big sister's man."

Pace winced. "I'm not Bitsy's or anyone else's man," he said. "And the child could be Del's. He doesn't suspect it's not, does he?"

Punzy pushed Pace down into a chair and plunked herself on his lap. She strung her arms around his neck.

"Of course not," she said. "Are you still sweet on Bitsy?"

"Nothing's happening or will be between me and your sister. "

"Then will you please take me to bed?"

Punzy kissed Pace on the lips and pushed her peppermint-tasting tongue into his mouth. Pace had not been with a woman since his brief encounter with Siempre Desalmado, and now he had no desire or reason to resist Punzy, so he did not.

16

Pace should have guessed that his taking up with Punzy would not sit well with Bitsy. He had just purchased a bottle of Barbancourt rum when Bitsy cornered him as he stepped out of Spike and Mike's Liquor Room in Bay St. Clement. She was wearing white overalls to accommodate more comfortably her increasingly protruding stomach and a faded black Are You Experienced? Jimi Hendrix T-shirt. Her uncombed hair fell loosely around her shoulders and she was not wearing make-up. Still, she looked lovely and healthy, Pace thought, except for an expression on her face that made her appear as if she had just slaughtered a rabbit and bitten off its head. The only missing element was a smear of the decapitated creature's blood around Bitsy's mouth and chin.

"You just had to go and bang Punzy, didn't you? Damn it, Pace Roscoe Ripley, you didn't give a second's thought about how it would make me feel. Bein' pregnant and all, I mean. My emotional quotient ain't two blips off the perilous line, anyway, and then I gotta get an earful from my daddy-complected little sister who's practically the only person I've confided in concernin' your probable complicity in the upcomin' Great Event, about how she and you are romantically involved and she's fast convincin' herself that you're the man of her just-past-adolescent dreams. For your information, this is the same shit she broadcast about that decrepit, washed-up lounge lizard Mexican boozehound had a hard eight won't work any more, so don't get carried away thinkin' you're so g.d. special."

Pace stood and stared at this wild-eyed, wild-haired harridan whose acquaintance he had no recollection of ever having made before. Bitsy was winded from delivering her diatribe and was breathing hard. Pearl-sized sweat beads decorated her forehead and her mouth was locked in a paralyzed snarl. He waited until she seemed to have regained her composure before he spoke.

"What do you mean 'practically'?"

Bitsy was puzzled. "Huh?" she squeaked.

"You said Punzy was practically the only person you confided in about us."

"Yeah, so?"

"I thought it was our understanding that the possibility of my complicity, as you put it, was our secret to protect Del. And don't forget your not playin' straight with me from the jump."

Bitsy stepped back and ran her white-coated tongue around her lips as if she were cleansing them of the last few drops of rabbit blood.

"Fuck it, Pace, I'm a girl."

"I guess my grandmama Marietta's Mob beau Marcello Santos was correct when he said, 'Three can keep a secret if two are dead.'"

"Leave Punzy be, Pace, is all I'm sayin'. She's damaged goods. You don't know the whole story and no matter what she might have told you about herself it couldn't be the half of it. Not only that but her crazy Aztec husband is due to come crashin' out of the jungle any minute. Punzy didn't tell you he'd be huntin' her ass down?"

"She only said she wasn't sure if he would or not."

"Well, he's comin', and knowin' Abstemio Cruz as I do, he'll sniff Punzy's cunt juice on your peckerwood pecker from a kilometer away."

"Thanks for the warning, Bitsy. Now I'll go back to the cottage and mix myself a mojito or two."

Pace walked past Bitsy and got into his Pathfinder. Just as he was about to turn the key in the ignition, Bitsy ran to the driver's side window and planted a kiss on the glass. Then she turned around and walked off. Pace sat there, confused, bewildered and dazed.

"All things bein' equal, Daddy," he said aloud, hoping Sailor might hear his lament, "they ain't now and never have been."

17

Abstemio Cruz was not about to let Punzy get away. He told his boss, Hugo Lengua, at La Pajarera, an upscale bar in the Hotel Habita in colonia Polanco, that there had been a death in his wife's family and that he needed a week off to be with her in North Carolina. The fact that Hugo Lengua was on the verge of firing him on account of his chronic tardiness and periodic vocal abuse of customers whom he felt were not appreciative enough of his musical stylings or choice of material did not occur to Cruz. Lengua granted Abstemio's request and privately decided to hire another singer-piano player while Cruz was away. If and when Abstemio returned, Hugo Lengua figured, if the new guy was working out, he'd give Cruz two weeks severance pay and wish him buena suerte. If Cruz gave him any trouble, Hugo would shoot him and have his cousin, Zoco Mochar, a top dog with the Sinaloa cartel, dispose of the body.

Cruz would have gone anyway, whether or not Lengua granted him permission. Punzy was his little blonde gringa goddess; without her, he believed, he would lose his inspiration, even his reason for living, and probably the last piece of perfect young pussy he would ever have.

Abstemio flew from Mexico City to Atlanta, then to Raleigh-Durham, where he rented a car at the airport. Driving toward Bay St. Clement, he thought about the three women who had been the most important in his early life: his mother, Dolores; his aunt, Tristessa; and his own sister, Alegría. Dolores, whose name in Spanish means pains, and her sister, Tristessa, whose name means sadness, had had very difficult lives, and together decided that Abstemio's sister should be named Alegría, which means joy and happiness, in the hope that she would have an easier existence than their own. Alegría had been a happy child, it was true, but at the age of six and a half she had been killed in a car wreck along with her father, Imprudente Ingrato. Abstemio was four at the time and thereafter bore the burden of having to endure his mother and aunt's impermeable mourning. Their bereavement was for Alegría only, not Imprudente, who by all accounts was a foolish loser, a bad gambler addicted to tequila and teenage whores. As a young man his good looks and proper manners gained him admirers and opportunities to succeed in business, but his increasingly bad habits and tawdry behavior prevented him from ever amounting to much. Barely sixteen years old when she married him, Dolores soon grew to hate him and would have been pleased had the accident taken only his life.

Abstemio bore the weight of Dolores and Tristessa's gloominess as well as he could but believed that his alcoholism and violent outbursts were a direct result of this condition. Rapunzelina, his fourth wife, was the brightness that had been missing since his sister's death, and he did not want to lose what his favorite writer, Ernesto Hemingway, had called the light at the end of the world. If he and Punzy ever had a daughter, he intended to name her Luz.

Abstemio promised himself that he would quit drinking and forcing Punzy to have rough sex with him once he took her back to Mexico City, but he had a flask filled with Havana Club rum packed in his suitcase and he needed a drink. Cruz pulled over onto the side of the highway and stopped the car. He got out and opened the trunk. Just as he had unlocked the suitcase, taken out the flask, unscrewed the cap and put the tip to his lips, a Highway Patrol car pulled up behind him. Two tall, beefy patrolmen got out, both wearing reflector shades, saw him taking a swig and drew their weapons.

"Santa María!" Abstemio Cruz said to them. "Por favor, if I am going to die, let it happen in my own country."

18

When Punzy asked Pace to accompany her to bail Abstemio Cruz out of jail in the country town of Nisbet, North Carolina, he wanted to refuse. It was almost midnight when she knocked on his door. Pace was reading *A Miracle of Catfish*, the last, unfinished novel by Larry Brown, a Mississippi writer who had died young. Brown, whom Pace had known and even gone squirrel hunting with one time, had been the kind of writer Pace would have liked to be had he the inclination and ability: surgically observant and understanding even of violent behavior absent any hint of false tenderness or rude exploitation. Locked into Larry's rural-elegant, unpanicked narrative, Pace resented Punzy's intrusion, knowing he was helpless not to acquiesce.

"What about Bitsy and Del?" he asked. "Did you tell them your husband was here? Or almost. And why is he in jail?"

Punzy was shaking and kept biting the tips of her fingers.

"They told me to leave him there," she said. "The cops got him for bein' drunk and disorderly and drunken driving. He says it ain't true. I need five hundred dollars to get him out."

Pace drove Punzy to Nisbet, where after some difficulty they located the jailhouse hidden behind a farm supply and feed store called Collier & Dexter's. He wrote a check for the five hundred and gave it to the night clerk, a porcine, completely hairless individual of indeterminate age wearing a pair of dark glasses missing one lens. The night clerk then ordered one of the patrolmen who'd arrested Abstemio Cruz to "Fetch your wetback." By this time it was past three o'clock in the morning.

Pace had had to show his driver's license and sign a guarantee to deliver the prisoner on a certain date to the courthouse in Raleigh. Until then, the Mexican national would be in Pace's custody.

"I'm not thrilled about this, Punzy," he said, while they waited for her husband to be brought out. "I hate to say it but I'm more than a little uncomfortable havin' him be my responsibility, especially if he decides to take off back to Mexico. If he bolts, I'll lose the five hundred plus another forty-five hundred they'll come after me for."

"I know you are, Pace, honey, and I'm really sorry to drag you into this, but what else could I do?"

Punzy bit harder into her fingers, one at a time, extending her neck as if she were a deer nibbling berries off a branch.

Abstemio Cruz appeared. The guard held him firmly by his left elbow. Cruz obviously had been roughed up; there were fresh bruises on his face and he staggered forward. He kept his head lowered as the tall patrolman removed his handcuffs, and when Cruz looked up at Punzy he curled the right side of his upper lip and snarled, "It is my wish that the whole human race had one neck and I had my hands around it."

"This un's an ornery beaner," the highway patrolman said. "I hope you know what you're doin'."

Rapunzlina took Cruz by one arm and walked him out of the jailhouse.

"Who are you to him?" the cop asked Pace.

"I am a pilgrim and a stranger," Pace said, then followed Punzy and her husband into the middle of the night.

Back at the house, Bitsy was awake and more than uncommonly unhappy about the situation. She and her sister began arguing immediately. Abstemio Cruz collapsed onto a couch in the front room and fell asleep despite the women's loud voices. Del was upstairs. Pace fled the shouting and snoring and walked to his cottage, wondering why he'd allowed himself to have gotten into this mess. He was about to open the screen door when he heard a shot. Punzy came running out of Dalceda's house and threw herself into Pace's arms.

"Oh, Lord Jesus, Del shot Bitsy!" she cried. "She told him the baby wasn't his!"

There was a second shot, then another. Pace and Punzy stood frozen, holding each other. The silence that followed was louder than any noise Pace had ever heard.

Finally, he said, "Wait here."

Pace walked slowly toward the house, knowing what he was about to see. He entered and there it was: after shooting Bitsy, Del had shot the slumbering Mexican and then himself. The three of them—four, counting Bitsy's unborn child— were dead. Pace heard a car engine start. He stepped out onto the porch in time to see Punzy speeding down the driveway in her sister's Subaru.

He sat down on the porch swing and remembered sitting there with Lula and his grandmama Marietta when he was a boy, waiting for Dalceda Delahoussaye to bring out the lemonade she made with cane sugar that he loved so much. The sky was brightening and the air was cool and moist. A fox ran across the lawn between the house and the cottage, quickly disappearing into the woods. A line of dialogue from an old black and white foreign movie popped into his head: "On this earth there is one thing that's terrible—it's that everyone has his reasons."

Pace swung gently back and forth until the sun was almost up before he got up and went back inside to call the police.

19

Because of the extraordinary nature of the circumstances, the hamlet of Nisbet returned to Pace the five hundred dollars he'd put up for Abstemio Cruz's bond. The police would have liked to talk to Punzy, but she had disappeared; and as she was not an eyewitness to the murders, her participation in the investigation was therefore deemed non-essential. Delbert Parker was declared to be the sole perpetrator of the incident and the case was closed.

To say the least, Pace was not eager for more company. He hoped that Rapunzelina would stay away forever and he decided to not rent Dalceda's house to anyone. Pace resolved to devote his energies to writing his story of Sailor and Lula. His involvement in the tragedy with the Parkers would no doubt haunt him always, Pace knew that, and he understood that he would have to accept a certain amount of responsibility for what occurred.

Pace considered himself fortunate that Del did not shoot him, too. The only reason Del probably did not come after him was that Bitsy had not indentified Pace as the man who had impregnated her. What was it Dr. Furbo had said about how to process regret? Pace had to find the Desirable Gap, the mental state whereby he could conceivably achieve an adequate degree of solace. He needed help, but Furbo was dead, as, of course, were Sailor and Lula. The only consolation for Pace was for him to continue his quest for the Up-Down.

For weeks after the shootings, Pace was unable to concentrate on his writing, the terrible event still too fresh a wound in his mind. Then, at two o'clock on an overcast afternoon, while he was reading around in the journals of André Gide, having just finished a passage wherein Gide declares, "Dostoyevsky's greatness lies in the fact that he never reduced the world to a theory, that he never let himself be reduced by a theory, whereas Balzac constantly sought a theory of passions; it was great luck for him that he never found it," the telephone rang in the cottage.

"Hello, Pace? It's me, Punzy. Can you talk?"

"I can, but I'm not sure I want to talk to you."

"Pace, I'm so sorry about buggin' out like I did. It was just all so horrible I needed to get away fast."

"Where are you?"

"Here."

"Where's 'here'?"

"Bay St. Clement. I'm gettin' gas at Oscarito's fillin' station. I still got Bitsy's Subaru. Poor Bitsy. Can I come see you?"

When Pace did not respond immediately, Punzy said, "Please? I won't stay if you think it's a bad idea. We need to talk, I think. I mean, I do. To explain. I miss bein' with you."

"Okay."

Pace thought about leaving before Punzy got there, but before he could even move she was standing in front of him.

"You cut your hair," he said.

"Joan of Arc," said Punzy, caressing the back of her neck with her right hand. "Do you like it?"

20

"I hid out in a cheap motel, Moke's, on Reno Street near the C-stock track where the kids I hung out with in high school would go to rent a room for seven bucks and get loaded. I was there for a week, then drove down to Savannah to bunk with an old beau of mine named Travis Chavis, who's turned gay now. His daddy owned the Kickin' Chicken chain of restaurants. Travis inherited a ton of money when he turned twenty-one and bought himself a mansion in the best part of town. Lives with his boyfriend, a black man named Devondre Williams-Williams used to be a star runnin' back at Georgia Tech until he got thrown off the team for detrimental behavior—Devondre told me he wore dresses and women's undergarments in the locker room—and lost his scholarship. Travis paid for his plastic surgery so now Devondre looks kind of like Katharine Hepburn with the physique of Arnold Schwarzenegger. He quit takin' steroids, though, 'cause they shrunk his private parts. Anyway, I didn't have any available cash so Travis took me in and then gave me a bunch when I decided to leave Savannah. I don't much like that town—they don't let dogs or even people walk on the grass in the parks there."

Punzy and Pace were sitting in facing armchairs in his cottage, drinking rum and Cokes. Pace wasn't sure what he should do about her; he was still attracted to Punzy but he knew she was forty miles of bad road. His weakness disgusted him and while she talked he was working up the nerve to send her on her way.

"When I was stayin' at Travis's, though, I thought deep and hard about how careless and foolish I've been with my one and only life. Devondre helped me out there, describin' his own self and discoverin' he couldn't handle goin' through the remainder of his time on earth without bein' the person he knew he really was. Of course I'd thought about this before, which is why I decided to become a nurse. I'm thinkin' I should go to Africa and help rid Sudanese or Congolese kids of all the diseases they got.

"Bitsy's and my daddy, Purvis Pasternak, was an evil man. I don't know if Bitsy told you about him. He owned a gun store in Charlotte where all the Klansmen, if there still is a Klan, hung out. When our mother, Martita Hunter, who was from Mississippi originally, died, I was eleven. Bitsy was just out of college. Daddy began molestin' me then, after Bitsy was gone to graduate school in Chapel Hill. She was so smart the colleges all paid to have her. Daddy told me it was what God intended, to keep the comminglin' of the sexes, as he called it, in the family. I guess he never done nothin' with Bitsy because Mama was still alive. When my sister'd come home for the holidays, he'd leave off foolin' with me until she'd go back to school. I got pregnant when I was thirteen so Daddy sent me to stay in a home for unwed mothers in St. Louis, The Saviors of All the King's Daughters it was called. When Bitsy came to see me there I told her it was our daddy who'd made me with child and she swore she'd never again go back to his house, and she never did. I had the baby, not knowin' if it was a girl or a boy, I didn't want to, and let The Saviors give it to an adoption agency, which they got paid for and didn't give me nothin' of it. I went back to Charlotte and when Daddy made a move to resume carryin' on with me I refused and told him I'd kill him in his sleep if he laid a hand on me. He kept away after that and done his business with black prostitutes he'd bring home late at night.

"I finished high school, where I got a reputation as a bad girl. In fact, I slept with boys, men and women, too, whoever wanted me. I didn't mind, so long as it wasn't Daddy. He got knifed by one of his whores and lost a kidney when I was in my last year. He didn't get no sympathy from me, and followin' graduation I went to junior college in Tallahassee, Florida, where Bitsy was livin'; that's where she met Del Parker. I guess I got bored there and took off with a stupid boy from New Orleans named Tosco Orchid to Mexico. He got sick in Mexico City and almost died from typhoid fever or somethin', so soon as he was recovered enough to travel again he went back to N.O. I stayed and got tangled up with Abstemio, whom I met while I was workin' illegally as a dance hostess in Tepito. He spent a lot of money on me and we got drunker than usual one night and I married him. You about know the rest."

"You can't stay here," Pace said. "I need to be by myself and finish the book I'm writing. Company won't cut it."

Punzy put her drink down on a side table, stood up so that he could appreciate her nifty figure, then stepped over to Pace and leaned down so that their noses almost touched.

"Tell me true you don't want to play Two-Cobras-in-a-Bag with me," she said.

Pace gently pushed Punzy away, rose from his chair and opened the front door.

"Please go, Punzy," he said. "I don't want to be mean, I just have to figure things out and I won't be able to if you're here."

Punzy dropped to her knees and began sobbing. Pace watched and listened to her heave and cry until he couldn't stand it any more and closed the door.

She looked up at Pace, smiled weakly and said, "I'll let my hair grow long again if you want me to."

*

21

Rapunzelina did her best to not be too much of a distraction to Pace. She went to the library in Bay St. Clement and did the proper research regarding gaining admission to nursing schools and very soon began sending out applications. When she wasn't at the library or running errands, such as buying groceries, Punzy spent most of her daytime hours in Dalceda's house, which is where she and Pace regularly had dinner. At night they slept together in the cottage. Pace's writing was going well and he was pleasantly surprised by Punzy's understanding of his need for privacy. Pace enjoyed their time together and, despite the sadness caused by the death of her sister, Punzy seemed genuinely happy.

Then one evening six months after her return, she did not show up back at the house and did not call. Pace fixed his own supper and afterwards went back to the cottage and read until he fell asleep. It was after two in the morning when Pace was awakened by loud noises coming from Dalceda's house. He looked out his bedroom window and saw the Subaru and a red Dodge Ram pick-up parked in the driveway. Lights were on in the big house and terrible techno music was blasting from it. Pace got up, put on his pants and shoes and went over to find out what was going on.

He found Punzy and two bearded, middle-aged men snorting lines of cocaine off a counter in the kitchen. One of the men had a patch over his left eye and was naked from the waist down. The other man was completely naked and was swigging from a fifth of Jack Daniel's in between inhaling coke through a rolled up twenty dollar bill. Punzy was fully dressed. Her eyes were only half open and she staggered over to a chair and passed out with her head on the table.

"Who're you?" shouted the man with an eyepatch when he noticed Pace. Before Pace could say anything, the other man began urinating on the floor. Pace took off and ran back to the cottage, grabbed his Remington .332 over-and-under shotgun and two shells from the bedroom closet, loaded the gun and walked quickly back to the house.

The two men were still in the kitchen. The one with the eyepatch was shaking Punzy by her right shoulder, trying to get her to wake up. His cock was at half-mast and he was yelling.

"Come on, honey gal, suck Porter's hairy old dick again!"

Pace leveled the shotgun at him and said, "Get out."

The other man threw his whisky bottle at Pace. It missed and Pace turned the .332 a few degrees and shot him in the groin. The man screamed and fell down.

"Take him and get out!" Pace shouted at Eyepatch, pointing the gun again at him.

Eyepatch lifted up his partner, who was howling and writhing in pain while bleeding copiously onto the floor, and dragged the wounded man out the back door. Pace stood in the doorway and watched as Eyepatch dumped him in the bed of the truck, then got behind the steering wheel and drove away.

The men's clothes were scattered around the kitchen. Pace

walked into the dining room and fired the other shell into Punzy's Bose, blowing it apart and off the table they had become used to having dinner on, then went back into the kitchen. Punzy had slid off her chair onto the floor, where her head rested in a pool of the wounded man's blood.

Pace sat down in the chair in which Rapunzelina had been sitting and placed the shotgun on the table. It was quiet now in the kitchen except for the gurgling sound of Punzy's troubled breathing. Words from the Fourth Circle of Dante's *Inferno* came to his mind and he spoke them:

"Not without cause our journey is to the pit."

Pace did not move for a very long time. He looked down again at Punzy and wondered what would become of her. Her breathing feathered out and she slept now like a child. Pace looked up and imagined Sailor was sitting across the table from him, smiling.

"Well, Daddy," Pace said. "I've got my answer now. You had Mama's everlasting arm to lean on and I don't. That was your secret, wasn't it? Havin' Lula there for you made it possible to go on."

Pace knew what he wanted to write now. He got up and walked back to the cottage.

Part Four

1

The one person Pace could think of that he wanted to see and whom he believed would understand his state of mind following the bizarre and highly unsettling events of the past few months was Marnie Kowalski. Marnie lived in New Orleans, and during his first few weeks back in the city in which he'd grown up, after his divorce from Rhoda Gombowicz, Pace and Marnie had been lovers; but their mutual saving grace was that they had become good friends into the bargain and remained close despite the waning of their short-lived romantic entanglement. Pace trusted Marnie and he knew she trusted him, so it was to Marnie Pace turned in his most recent of darkest hours.

"Pace, it's so good to hear your voice. I'm glad you're callin' 'cause I've thought of you often since you moved to North Carolina. How're things, darlin'?"

"Marnie, you know I've seen and gone through some more than passin' strange episodes in my life but lately there've been several goin's on have about got me puzzled as to God's plan."

Marnie laughed and said, "Pace, honey, you of all people know He ain't never had one. Don't give me any details 'til you get here. You are comin' to see me, aren't you? Isn't that why you're callin' now? Not that you'd ever have to phone first, you know."

"Thanks, Marnie, yes. It's good you're still so prescient

about most things. I'd like to get back to N.O. for a little while and I was hopin' you'd be up for takin' me in. If anything, Bay St. Clement ain't turned out to be any more peaceful than anywhere else. I'm writin', though, and that seems to be pretty much holdin' my mind together. What about you?"

"I opened a bakery over on St. Philip. Goin' pretty good so far. I call it Kowalski's Cake & Pie Company. Open from five A.M. 'til two P.M.; then I go swimmin' at the Y. What're you writin'?"

"The story of Sailor and Lula; it's a novel."

"Can't wait to read it, babe. When you comin'?"

"It'll take me a couple of days to close up the houses and pay some bills. I'll drive over once that's done. Now you got me thinkin' about your lemon meringue pie. Nobody in N.O. besides you could ever get it to come out right."

"People don't understand the weather here like I do, that's why. It's the weather affects the bakin'. Well, this is Sunday, so I'll be expectin' you around Thursday. If I'm not at the house I'll probably be at the bakery, corner of St. Philip and Burgundy."

"Thanks, Marnie. You know I love you to death."

"Love you to death, too, Pace. Drive careful."

Pace hung up. The last time he'd seen her, Marnie was living with two rescued and supposedly rehabilitated pit bulls she'd named Milk and Honey. She had a boyfriend, too, an ex-Navy Seal—Bigger or Digger, Marnie called him, Pace couldn't remember. He wondered if that guy was still around. Marnie hadn't mentioned him.

Pace was not entirely certain that he should be leaving at all, but he did feel the need to create some distance for himself from the killings and reprehensible behavior of Rapunzelina Pasternak Cruz. Where she had gone Pace did not know and did not want to know. Perhaps she would make it to the Congo one of these days and do some good for mankind like she hoped, though Pace had his doubts.

The night before he left for N.O., Rapunzelina appeared to Pace in a dream. She was naked, adorned only by numerous bracelets on each arm, rings on every one of her fingers and indecipherable tattoos on her breasts. Punzy extended her arms toward him, turned upward the palms of her hands and said, "Do not forgive me. The river is mine and I have made it."

2

Driving to New Orleans, Pace realized that the route he was following from Bay St. Clement was the same one his mother and her lifelong best friend, Beany, had taken on the last trip of Lula's life. At the age of eighty she had gone on the road to visit Pace, which she had, and stayed with Beany at Marnie Kowalski's house on Orleans Street. All had gone relatively well until a dilemma in Beany's family caused the women to cut short their time with Pace. It was on their way to Beany's daughter's home in Plain Dealing, Louisiana, that Lula suffered a heart attack and died.

Lula and Beany had encountered a spot of trouble in South Carolina after a young man they had given a ride to was stabbed to death by a disturbed woman he met during a stopover. Both Lula and Beany had been unnerved by this incident but Pace did not think it had anything to do with his mother's subsequent passing. Lula had experienced many worse situations in her lifetime and managed to weather them all. Her heart, strong and wild as it was, had finally just quit. Pace missed his parents but was satisfied that they had lived their lives as best they could and passed on to him their spirit of adventure, decency and generosity. As far as legacies go, Pace figured, that was about as good as one could get.

By the time Pace arrived at Marnie's late Thursday afternoon, he was exhausted both mentally and physically. He had stopped on the way only to sleep, eat and get gas, keeping conversation with anyone, such as the motel clerk, waitress or station attendant to a minimum. As soon as he had parked his Pathfinder on Orleans Street, two houses down from Marnie's, Pace fell asleep in the driver's seat and did not wake up until Ms. Kowalski herself knocked on the front passenger side window.

"Pace Ripley! Here I am, darlin', the one you can't live without."

Pace opened his eyes and saw his old friend standing on the sidewalk grinning at him through the glass. The sun had gone down and Marnie's short blonde hair glowed in the gray-green light of the New Orleans evening. He got out of the car and embraced her.

"It's true," Pace said. "Other than the unlikely event of Sailor and Lula bein' resurrected, there ain't nobody on the planet other than you whose company I believe I could tolerate."

Marnie laughed and said, "That either don't speak so highly of the human race or of you, Mr. Ripley, sir. Which is it?"

"I'm tryin' to decide."

Pace picked up the few belongings he'd brought with him and followed Marnie into her house. Milk and Honey barked furiously at the sight of him, so Marnie put them out into the yard.

"What about Bigger, or Digger, or whatever his name is?"

"Digger's on his fifth tour of duty in Afghanistan. I don't expect him back for another six months. That's if he makes it back, of course."

"A lot can happen in six months, Marn."

"Sure as shit," she said.

Marnie removed two Abita Ambers from her refrigerator, opened them, and handed one to Pace. They clinked bottles. Marnie took a swig, grinned and said, "And I'm hopin' somethin' will."

Pace swallowed half the contents of his bottle and smiled back.

"Did the thought ever occur to you, fine progeny of Sailor Ripley and Lula Fortune, that everybody's dodgin' bullets one way or another whether they know it or not?"

"It's a good thing for us then that most folks can't shoot straight."

Marnie sidled up to Pace, kissed him softly on the lips, and said, "Think you could give me a straight shot where I need it the most?"

"Right now?"

"Rat now, as my Grandmama Elsie Buell in Nacogdoches used to say, bless her heart. I do believe history is still made at night."

As Pace followed Marnie up the stairs to her bedroom, he recalled his daddy telling him that once when he was in high school following a girl up a flight of stairs like this Sailor reached up, put a hand between her legs and the girl turned and said, "Oh, what a bad boy you are."

Pace put his right hand between Marnie's legs and without stopping she cooed, "I never could get enough of you bad boys."

In her bedroom Marnie pulled down the shade over the window facing Orleans Street, then threw her arms around Pace's neck.

"Tell me, darlin'," Marnie said, "don't it feel like home?"

3

It was two o'clock in the morning and Pace was lying in Marnie's bed listening to Etta Jones sing "Don't Go to Strangers" on the radio. "When you need more than company," she suggested, "don't go to strangers, come on to me." Pace had always loved this song and Etta's tangy delivery, the way she let it curl gently into the night air. He also dug Skeeter Best's dignified guitar solo, not subtle but unobtrusive, just right, which was the way Pace felt this very moment. It was the first time he'd been able to relax since the insane series of events occasioned by his dealings with the Pasternak sisters. A remarkably cool breeze from the river snaked in through the slightly open bedroom window, causing Pace to pull a sheet up over his chest. The thought hit him that he had not felt really peaceful since leaving N.O., and he had to come back to get it. Etta Jones' final soft figure segued into Willis "Gator Tail" Jackson on tenor playing "This'll Get To Ya" with Brother Jack McDuff filling on organ. Marnie was downstairs in the kitchen making omelettes for them. They had not eaten dinner, having fallen deeply asleep after making love. Pace savored the moment. Craziness was never far from home, wherever that might be, but you didn't have to sign up for it. He closed his eyes and shivered a little from the breeze. When he reopened them, Marnie, completely naked except for a leopard print scarf tied around her neck, walked through the doorway holding two plates.

"Guess what, darlin'?" she said. "Day after tomorrow I'm puttin' you to work in the bakery."

4

Pace didn't have much time to write. He'd never baked a cake in his life, so he had to learn from scratch. Marnie put him to work making Magdalena Kowalski's Krakow yellow cake, named after her mother, from Magdalena's recipe. Pace enjoyed doing the basic preparation, measuring the dry ingredients, sifting the cake flour, then re-sifting it with the baking powder and salt, creaming the butter and sugar, adding egg yolks (never the whole egg), vanilla and grated lemon rind—using both, Marnie explained, was her mother's secret—and adding the sifted ingredients to the butter mixture in three parts with thirds of milk. After Pace had poured this into pans prepared with parchment and put them into the oven, he left the filling and frosting to Marnie or her second in command, Dolores Silva, a native of Jalisco, Mexico, who had lived illegally in the United States for forty years, since she was ten. Her parents and grandparents had all been great cooks and passed their collective culinary knowledge on to Dolores. Marnie told Pace that Dolores made the best white pozole on the planet, and he was eager to try it whether or not he had a hangover.

While Marnie went swimming in the afternoons, Pace usually took a nap, then wrote for a couple of hours before having a cocktail with her. They had dinner together and went to bed early. After four weeks of this routine, Pace felt renewed, the poison of the previous months having drained from his system almost entirely. Other than taking Milk and Honey out to run in Toni Jones Park behind Dillard University, Marnie and Pace stayed close to home. This suited Pace and he and Marnie got along with "nary a ripple" as she said old Elsie Buell would have put it.

Pace was awakened from his nap on a Thursday afternoon by Marnie, who came into the bedroom holding a sheet of paper and an envelope. She sat down in a rocking chair next to the bed and shook her head from side to side.

"What's up, Marn? Why aren't you at the Y?"

"Special delivery letter arrived just as I was goin' out the door. Digger got blown up by an incendiary explosive device along with three other guys in a jeep on the outskirts of Kabul. Those three are dead. Digger survived but he lost a leg—it doesn't say which one—and was permanently blinded. He's already in D.C. at a rehab center. They're gonna release him this Saturday and fly him to N.O. I've got to take him in, Pace. He's got no place else to go."

"Of course you do."

"It says in the letter that he'll continue his rehabilitation at the VA hospital here, but he can live at home. I'm afraid this puts an A-number one crimp in our own arrangement, at least for the time bein'."

Marnie's eyes were full of tears; certainly for poor Digger, but probably, Pace thought, partially for the abrupt cessation of his and her newfound idyll.

"What's Digger's real name?" he asked.

"Francisco Madero Bernstein. His daddy was a scholar of the Mexican revolution. Taught at Stanford University, I believe."

"You'll visit me sometime in North Carolina, I hope."

Marnie smiled and let her tears fall.

"Of course I will, darlin'."

"If you let me know when you're comin'," Pace said, "I'll bake a cake."

5

Since childhood Pace had been interested in people's stories about their interaction with extraterrestrials. Most of these accounts were ludicrous if not patently ridiculous, of course, but occasionally someone sounded convinced that he or she had actually been contacted by or had some sort of relation with emissaries from planets other than Earth. Pace rarely read science fiction or watched television shows or movies that involved space travel. What fascinated him was personal testimony, hearing people talk about their intimate experiences with aliens. Usually these individuals could be heard on radio programs in the middle of the night, telling how small gray or tall blue beings, some without mouths or with three eyes, had appeared in barns on isolated farms or kidnapped the subject and taken him to their own planet to experiment upon. Often these witnesses or participants sounded so sincere that Pace knew they believed what they were saying. Delusional or not, Pace remained curious as to what transpired in these people's minds to allow them to describe in such vivid detail their unearthly experiences.

Sitting at the desk in his cottage late at night, or lying awake in bed, Pace acknowledged to himself that he would not mind having an encounter of the third kind, as such contacts were called. If he was taken away to another galaxy it would unburden him from trying to figure out a reason for existence. Not that he expected to be given or have revealed to him an explanation; it would be enough, Pace decided, to know there was more than one answer or no answer. Pace did not believe in God, he never had, but he understood why doing so was a comfort to so many people. He just enjoyed the idea of going somewhere else, someplace unimaginable.

When he received a letter from Marnie three months after he'd returned to Bay St. Clement, telling him that she had married Digger and was bound to devote herself to his well-being for however long that might be, Pace was not surprised, but for a moment he wished he were on another planet.

6

Pace was walking through a field of high grass in the woods a quarter of a mile from Dalceda Delahoussaye's house on a cold, cloudy December day, thinking about what most significantly could have occupied Lula's thoughts during her last fifteen years, the ones without Sailor. His parents' undying trust in one another was what Pace admired most about them. There were certain people he trusted, of course, Marnie being one, and he had trusted his ex-wife, Rhoda, too; but it was not the same because the bond between Sailor and Lula had endured what for them had been forever.

A six-point buck came thundering through the grass and passed from right to left directly in front of Pace. Before its odor reached his nostrils and before he heard the shot, a bullet entered just to the right and slightly below Pace's left shoulder blade. He turned and saw a man wearing eyeglasses and an orange hat with earflaps about fifty yards behind him. The man was holding a rifle. He stood still for a few seconds, then began running away from Pace, toward a dense thicket. Pace reached around with his right hand and tried to touch the spot where the projectile had penetrated his back but he could not find it. Before he fell, Pace looked again for the man wearing an orange hat but he was gone. Lying in the tall grass, Pace stared up at the gathering grey clouds and thought, if ever there were a time for him to be abducted by aliens, this was it.

7

The supervising nurse in the critical care unit of Nuestra Hermana de Perdón Hospital in South Nazareth, where Pace had been taken to recover from his wounds, was named Anita O'Day O'Shea, whom everyone on the hospital staff called Lady O. Lady O was seventy-six years old and in her fifty-fifth year of service. Still vigorous, sharp-minded and tart-tongued as ever, her expertise was well-respected by doctors and nurses alike. It was she who oversaw Pace's case and was the only person with whom he was allowed by the doctors to have a conversation. These exchanges were necessarily brief and consisted mostly of Lady O's relating to Pace her theory regarding spacecraft having landed on Earth thousands of years before, as recorded in the Book of Ezekiel in the Old Testament.

"Ezekiel was a son of Bunzi, a priest, and he witnessed the heavens open and from out of a fiery cloud came an amber-colored spaceship. Four four-winged creatures appeared, walking upright, each with four faces: one a man's, one a lion's, one an ox's, and one an eagle's. Their vehicle was metallic and formed in the shape of a wheel. When Ezekiel told the elders of Israel about this visitation, they refused to believe him and he was exiled to Babylonia. Mind you, this was around 600 B.C., so there's the first reliable proof that men from outer space been checkin' out our planet since forever. You feelin' better today, son?"

The bullet that pierced Pace had traveled through his back into his heart and exited from his chest. That he had survived was, in the words of the head surgeon at Nuestra Hermana de Perdón, a freak event. Lady O called it a miracle, a sign that God had plans for Pace.

"This is His way of tellin' you you got work left to do, Mr. Ripley," said Lady O. What that might be, I can't pretend to know, but He don't spare folks for no bad reason."

"I don't consider myself a Christian," Pace told her. "I don't hold much for organized religion of any kind, though I respect your beliefs and I am thoroughly grateful for your encouragement as well as your ministrations and devotion to my well-being."

During the earliest stage of his recovery, Pace had been under heavy sedation and had experienced an alternately entertaining and troubling, if not horrifying at times, series of dreams. In one, he found himself being devoured by an enormous crocodile, helpless to prevent it; but then Pace became the crocodile, gorging himself on a Chinese girl, a child, really, swallowing her head first, watching her legs kick until her top parts were chomped to bits. In another, Pace was in a city that was a combination of Paris, France, and Chicago; it was winter, snow was falling, and he wandered through the dimly-lit streets until he saw a woman he thought was Siempre Desalmado getting into a taxi. Pace ran after the taxi but he could not catch up. It disappeared and he fell down in the road and was soon covered by snow.

When at last his dreams became less intense, Pace forced himself to recall what happened, that he had been gunned down in the woods in a hunting accident but had somehow survived. When Lady O asked Pace if a bullet through his heart could not kill him, what could? Sailor and Lula's only child said, "That's not the only question I don't have the answer to."

Pace spent five weeks in the hospital before returning to Bay St. Clement. A private caregiver, Addie Mae Longbow, a septuagenarian, half-Cherokee woman who had worked with Lady O for a number of years before retiring from full-time nursing, attended Pace for almost a month, after which time he was able to take care of himself. Though still not at full strength, Pace got around well enough, he could drive and prepare his own meals. He resumed writing but resolved to do something for the good of others, to devote a portion of what energy he had to charity work. This desire did not stem from any righteous or empty feeling; it was just that Pace felt a considerable amount of disgust at what he deemed selfish, wasteful and narcissistic behavior, including his own. Fear, he concluded, was what drove people to behave as they did, and fear took many forms. Pace could not claim to be free of fear, but for whatever reason he felt less afraid than he ever had before.

Addie Mae Longbow was a member of an organization based in a warehouse in North Nazareth called Jesus Sees Us, which fed, clothed and provided free medical care to anyone in need. Pace donated three afternoons and evenings a week to Jesus Sees Us, serving lunch and dinner. It was while dishing up mashed potatoes and gravy on a Thursday evening three months after he had begun helping out there that Pace recognized the man wearing glasses and an orange hat with earflaps who had shot him.

Pace said nothing to the man as he passed in the serving line and then carried his food tray to a table, where he sat down and began to eat. Pace had had only a momentary glimpse of the delinquent hunter, but was certain this was he. As Pace continued to dole out potatoes, he kept an eye on the person who had plugged him and fled, trying to decide what to do. When the man in the orange hat finished eating and got up to go, Pace noticed that both of the lenses in his eyeglasses had cracks in them and that his green army field jacket was torn and dirty. As Pace watched him walk out of the dining area, the tension that had overcome him upon spotting the man gradually drained from his body. Pace felt not unlike he imagined Lazarus must have once he understood that he was truly again among the living.

"Mister, ain't you gonna spoon me some of them smashed 'taters?"

Pace looked at the stooped old woman in the line standing across from him, waiting to be served. Her deeply creased face and grizzled gray hair were filthy but there remained a distinct beam of brightness in her chestnut eyes.

"I surely am, ma'am," Pace said, scooping potatoes onto her plate. "Do you want gravy?"

9

It was early on a Sunday morning when Pace heard a car drive onto the property and stop. He looked out the front window of his cottage and saw a white Chevrolet Malibu parked between the cottage and Dalceda Delahoussaye's house. A woman climbed out of the driver's side, opposite the cottage, and stood for a moment with her back to him, shaking her long, blonde hair. He felt a chill in his back and shoulders and shivered even before the woman turned and faced his way. It was Rapunzelina Cruz, appearing in Pace's life for the third time.

She saw Pace behind the window, smiled and raised her right hand and gave a little wave. Pace did not acknowledge her overture. He could not move. Punzy may not have been the last person Pace expected to see but she was close. He did not want to be there with Punzy waiting for him to invite her inside. She looked almost too beautiful standing next to the white Malibu, a light breeze wrinkling her little blue dress, the sunlight purifying her, as if this image could be enough to cleanse from his brain those terrible, indelible pictures housed there. When Pace made no sign of welcome, Punzy's smile faded and she waited until it became clear to her that he was not going to allow her to interrupt his existence this time around. After a couple of minutes, Punzy got back into the car, started it up and backed down the driveway.

Once the Malibu was out of sight and sound, Pace thought about the importance of confronting one's demons, the man in the orange hat and Rapunzelina being only two transitory tests of his resolve and understanding. Pace then considered the possibility that the manifestations of both the hunter and Punzy might have been apparitions. If he had learned anything, he reasoned, what was the difference, really? He had let them go, and that was what mattered.

Part Five

1

On the eve of Pace's seventieth birthday, he realized that he had been living alone for almost eleven years. Not since his brief residence with Marnie Kowalski in New Orleans, which had followed the debacle that was his relationship with Rapunzelina Cruz, did he have any real interest even in keeping steady company with a woman. Pace was regular in his habits, maintained his writing routine, adding steadily to his monumental meditation—currently in excess of two thousand manuscript pages—on the lives of Sailor and Lula, and did what work needed to be done around the cottage and Dalceda Delahoussaye's house. It was practically a hermit's existence; other than necessary exchanges with shopkeepers in Bay St. Clement and periodic telephone conversations with Marnie, who was now beginning her second decade of marriage to Digger Bernstein, Pace eschewed personal relations. To his surprise, after so many years of being at the very least a nominally social being and world traveler, Pace discovered that he preferred this solitude. To be left alone was not the worst of circumstances; not by far, he reasoned, especially as it had been largely his own doing.

Dalceda and her husband, Louis, had acquired during

their lifetime a rather interesting, if eclectic, library, and during these last several years Pace had read many of the books they had accumulated. Louis, it seemed, had a taste for poetry, most particularly ancient Chinese verse in English translation, along with a complementary collection of books on Asian art. Pace had met Dalceda's husband only a couple of times, he had died when Pace was still a child, and this seemed a good way to get to know Louis Delahoussaye, through his library.

A poem that Pace came upon in one of the Chinese anthologies, attributed to an unknown poet of the T'ang dynasty who had been a government official before being exiled as a result of a political scandal to a remote province in the mountains, where he lived by himself until his death, particularly impressed Pace:

READING IN THE STUDY IN
THE BAMBOO GROVE

Lonely for conversation,
the scholar in the mountain hut
goes on reading.

Pace identified with the poem and it continued to resonate for him more than any others. Marnie, he knew, would call the next day to wish him a happy birthday and invite him, as she often did, to visit her and Digger in N.O. He would be pleased to hear her voice and would thank her for remembering the occasion, and decline the invitation for now. Perhaps later in the year, he would offer, and Marnie would counter with, "We're not gettin' any younger." This he knew and did not mind knowing. In fact, Pace had written a poem that succinctly expressed his view of the landscape:

LITTLE MIDNIGHT BUDDHIST POEM

Don't take
your Self
so seriously
Remove the I
from I don't mind
you have
Don't mind
which, after
All, is all
you'll need
or ever
have

2

On Pace's birthday, Marnie called, but it was to tell him that her husband, Francisco Madero "Digger" Bernstein, had died in his sleep three nights before.

"I guess it's too soon to ask you how you're feelin', now Digger's gone."

"Oh, I'm all right. He needed me and truly appreciated my doin' for him. I'll have time to take up some other things now."

"What about the bakery?"

"I got a couple of women run things there pretty good these days. It's still popular. Happy birthday, by the way."

"Thanks. You're the only one knows about it any more."

"You finish that book yet?"

"Might never will. I keep writin' on it, like Proust did on his, even on his deathbed."

"I hope you'll let me read some of it one of these days."

"I will, Marnie, I promise. Thanks for callin'. Sorry about Digger."

"You were really great about our havin' to part after he got blown up. Am I ever gonna see you again?"

"I have a sincere feelin' you will."

"What're you doin' to celebrate beginnin' your seventh decade on the planet?"

"It's strange thinkin' about how I've now outlived Sailor

Ripley by five years. Anyway, I'm about to go into town and buy myself a bottle of good single malt Scotch. The Glenmorangie Quinta Ruban, if they've got it."

"Maybe next year we can celebrate together."

Pace drove into Bay St. Clement, stopped in the liquor store and bought the only bottle of Glenmorangie they had. When he walked back outside, he noticed a sign on a door in a building across the street that read: CRUSADER RALPH's FOLLOWERS. He'd heard or read something about this bunch, men and women from all over the world who subscribed to the teachings of a former mercenary soldier who had escaped from prison in Mali, where he'd been sentenced to death for attempting to assassinate the president of that African country on behalf of a tribal warlord who opposed the government's ties to Al Qaeda. The president had branded Ralph as a CIA operative and it was most likely the CIA that had helped him get away. Supposedly he now lived on an undisclosed island in the South Pacific from where he communicated to his followers exclusively via the internet. Pace knew little else about Crusader Ralph, as the man began calling himself after fleeing Mali, and he was surprised to learn that the ex-merc's influence now extended to a little town in North Carolina.

When he got back to his cottage, Pace checked out Crusader Ralph on his computer. There wasn't much information available on the man's website, only a notice that said for an admission fee of five hundred dollars a person could submit him or herself for consideration to become eligible to receive the teachings, along with instructions for making payment. Pace then went to Wikipedia and read what it said there about Crusader Ralph: "According to his Followers, Crusader

Ralph is the one True Teacher in the universe. Other than he is believed to have been born in Akron, Ohio, no facts about his life are available and his Followers are forbidden to divulge his teachings to those outside the organization. For further reference go to www.crusaderralph.com."

Pace decided to visit the storefront in Bay St. Clement and find out what was behind the door, but not until after he'd had a birthday shot of single malt Scotch.

3

The next afternoon, Pace drove back into town, parked in the liquor store lot, walked across the street and knocked on the door with the Crusader Ralph's Followers sign on it. There was no immediate response, so Pace turned the knob but the door was locked. He knocked again and after thirty seconds an exotic-looking, ruby-skinned woman opened it. She was short and slender, middle-aged, perhaps in her late forties, with long, silky black hair and very large, oblong dark brown eyes set wide apart. She was wearing blue jeans and a pink T-shirt with the words I FOLLOW RALPH. DO YOU? printed on the front in white lettering.

"May I help you?" she asked.

"Did anyone ever tell you that you have eyes like Merle Oberon's?"

"No. Who is Merle Oberon?"

"An actress. She was a big movie star in the 1930s and '40s. Did you ever see *Wuthering Heights* with Laurence Olivier as Heathcliff and Merle Oberon as Cathy? Emily Brontë?"

The woman stared at Pace without blinking.

"My name is Pace Ripley and I want to know about Crusader Ralph."

"What is it you wish to know?"

"I might be interested in his teachings."

"Here is the teaching for today: 'Women always know what they want.' My name is Misty Tonga."

She closed the door.

Pace stood motionless on the sidewalk. He was amused and puzzled. Misty Tonga had not asked him for five hundred dollars but had given him a teaching anyway. Who was she? Pace considered knocking again on the door but instead decided he needed a beer and headed for the liquor store.

Pace bought a single tall boy of Dark Victory Ale and asked the clerk, a pimply, pudgy guy with glasses who was taking small bites out of a powdered doughnut, what, if anything, he knew about Crusader Ralph's Followers who had apparently set up shop across the street.

"Nothin'," said the clerk. "Do good works and the rest shall follow. That's all there is to study on."

Pace sat behind the steering wheel of his twelve-year-old Pathfinder sipping the Dark Victory.

"What about men?" he asked himself. "Why don't men always know what they want? Or maybe, according to Crusader Ralph, they do, too. Misty Tonga didn't say Ralph said they don't."

That evening, as Pace was preparing his dinner—chicken parmesan and salad—he listened on the radio to WSUP from Garden City, South Carolina, an African-American religious station familiarly called Wassup? —as in What's up? —although the call letters had originally been chosen as a reference to the Last Supper. When Pace tuned in, a visiting preacher from Norway was speaking.

"So when John and Peter entered the tomb where Jesus had been buried, they found the body gone, only His shroud shredded on the ground, an imitation of which garment later turned up in Turin. Thereafter, they propagated the myth that He was risen, resurrected, and sent Mary Magdalene, who had been waiting outside in the Jerusalem rain, to run and tell their fellow believers.

"Now let the truth be known: It was Jesus's true, biological father, Pantera—which means panther—retired from the Roman army, who had arrived first to claim the body and had taken it away. Jesus's mother, Mary, was thirteen when the soldier encountered her as she was returning from the well. Her husband, Joseph, who was much older than she, was away in the hills tending his flock of sheep. Mary and Pantera, who was but sixteen years old at the time of their meeting, became lovers before his legion was ordered to march.

"When months later Joseph came home and found his wife with child, she invented her wild story for fear of his wrath. He then spread the word of an immaculate conception, even though Mary's mother and sisters knew the truth. Mary swore them to secrecy and they did not betray her. After Jesus was grown and had begun to gain the reputation that eventually would doom him, Pantera, who had been off to the wars, heard the story. He remembered Mary and sought her out, whereupon she admitted that Jesus was his son.

"Pantera kept himself apprised of Jesus's career and in the end made away with his son's corpse. He took the body to Egypt, where he had it mummified and hidden. It was stolen, along with many examples of the ancient art, by British anthropologists and lodged in a museum in Liverpool, where it remained, unidentified, for decades. At some point, the museum had a fire and several of the exhibits were destroyed, among them the mummies. Though damaged, Jesus's mummified self was miraculously preserved. He was put onto a cart to be repaired but disappeared.

"It has only recently come to light, following a veritable variety of vicissitudes, and, due to modern methods of scientific detection, verified that this mummy, the remains of Jesus Christ, true son of Mary of Nazareth and The Panther of Rome, resides in the Hans Downe Museum of Medical Marvels in Oslo! I, Reverend Laiüs Downe, great-great grandson of the glorious explorer, doctor and distinguished professor after whom the museum is named, invite you to come to Norway to see it!"

Shouts and cries of joy and wonder ensued, congregants howling, "Praise the Lord!" and "Glory be to God!" An organist began playing "What A Friend We Have In Jesus," which the worshippers, punctuating with whoops and hollers, sang in unison. Loudest of all, since he retained use of the microphone on the pulpit, was the Reverend Laiüs Downe, inveighing unsonorously in his eerily high, Scandinavian-accented voice. Pace turned off the radio.

He carried his dinner plates to the kitchen table and sat down. Man's greatest weapon, Pace thought, is his imagination, but he doesn't always know where to point it.

4

Pace had to admit to himself that Misty Tonga interested him. He had for the most part shunned having anything to do with a woman that could have potentially resulted in an extended relationship—a word he despised almost as much as "awesome"—since Marnie Kowalski; and the thought of having to deal with a much younger woman had burned a hole in his cerebral cortex, an incendiary disaster delivered courtesy of the Cruz girl. Pace fought the feeling of wanting to check out Misty Tonga again, but a few days after first encountering her he returned to the entrance to Crusader Ralph's Followers and knocked on the door. This time, even after repeated attempts to summon someone, nobody answered. Pace tried the knob but, as before, the door was locked.

Pace was mildly disappointed and he felt restless, so he walked down the street and entered Duguid's Grill and Bar. It had been a long time, two years or more, Pace figured, since he'd been in Duguid's. The original owner's daughter, Rima Dot Duguid, had been in the movies for a while, then vanished from public view. Pace wondered what happened to her. He took a seat at the bar and looked around. It was just after two o'clock in the afternoon on a Tuesday, past the regular lunch hour, so only one of the six tables was occupied, and he was alone at the bar. At least he thought he was until to his genuine surprise Misty Tonga came out from the ladies' room and sat down four stools to his right. Pace had not noticed the drink on the bar in front of her. The bartender, a tall, thin but potbellied man with a dyed black mustache and bald head, came over to Pace and asked him what he'd have.

Pace nodded in the direction of Misty Tonga and asked him, "Is she drinking a White Russian?"

"She is. A double."

"I'll have one, too."

"Your funeral," said the bartender.

Misty Tonga was wearing black jeans and a black T-shirt with the same words on it as the pink one had. She did not give evidence of having noticed Pace, but after the double White Russian was set in front of him he picked it up, moved down the bar and stood behind the stool next to hers.

"Hello, Misty Tonga," he said, "remember me? Pace Ripley? From the other day? I just knocked on your door but nobody answered."

Only her eyes moved his way. She lifted her glass and took a sip of her drink. Pace studied her left profile. In the semi-darkness of the room her ruby-red flesh glowed.

"Did you come for another teaching?" she asked.

"Not really. But I was surprised you gave me one for free."

"What I told you was not a teaching. I just said that to make you go away."

Misty took another sip of her White Russian. Pace sat down.

"In this soft light," he said, "your skin looks like it's on fire."

"Did Merle Oberon have skin like mine?"

Pace grinned and said, "I don't think so, although I never saw her in person. Are you the only one who works in the Crusader Ralph office?"

"You haven't tried your drink."

"I haven't had a White Russian since I was in my twenties."

He picked up his glass, took a sip, winced a little, and set it back down on the bar.

"Too sweet for you," said Misty. "For me, too, actually. I order one every now and then to remind myself of a man who once told me my pussy smelled like a White Russian. I was twenty-two years old then. I'd never had one so I didn't know what it was. I thought he meant a woman from Russia."

"Where are you from, Misty?"

"Hacienda Heights, California."

She turned and looked into Pace's eyes.

"How old are you?" she asked.

"Pretty damn old. Seventy."

"I'm forty-six. Do you find me attractive? I mean, attractive enough to want to take me to bed?"

"Yes, Misty, I do."

She smiled and finished her drink, then she stood up.

"You've made me very happy, Mr. Ripley. I hope we will meet again."

Pace watched Misty Tonga walk out of the bar. The bartender came over.

"That woman's been comin' in here at about two o'clock every day for the last three weeks. Orders a White Russian, takes fifteen minutes to finish it, and goes. She's a woman of mystery."

"Seems to be," Pace said. "But she knows what she wants."

"Women always do."

"You happen to know whatever happened to Rima Dot Duguid, daughter of the people used to own this place?"

"Wasn't she a lion tamer or somethin' like that?"

"She played one in a movie once. She was an actress."

Pace picked up his glass but hesitated before taking another sip.

"That'll be five bucks whether you drink it or not," said the bartender.

Pace nodded, held the White Russian up to his nose, and sniffed it.

5

The sky looked like it was about to pour the afternoon Pace found the letter from Early Ripley addressed to him in his mailbox. He read the return address walking back to his cottage from the road: 127 Riverside Drive, New York, N.Y. Pace had never met his cousin Early, only heard his name a few times when Sailor had occasion to mention his second cousin Curly Ripley, who had gotten in some kind of fix involving gun running to Peru or somewhere and then dropped out of sight. Early, Pace believed, was Curly's son. Needless to say, Pace was more than a little surprised to have a letter from him, and opened the envelope as soon as he was inside the cottage.

"Dear Cousin Pace Roscoe, I'm sure this letter—if you receive it—coming from a relative stranger (Get it?) will certainly have been unexpected given the fact of our never having met or communicated during the course of our lives. I only recently learned that you were living in Bay St. Clement while doing research on the website trackem-n-hackem.com. You probably don't know it but our daddies lost touch with one another after my father, Lester 'Curly' Ripley, took me and my mother, Darla McFarland Ripley, with him to South America. I was seven years of age then and so you and I never had a chance to get to know each other, though somehow with all of my family's moving around in foreign lands during my young childhood Curly did his best to keep in touch with his mother, my grandmama Maybelline Napoleon, from the other side of the family. She told him what she knew of your daddy's doings, even his going to prison for killing a guy before he married your mama. I guess Curly and Sailor were buddies when they were real little.

"I don't know if you're interested in this talk about the past. I am seventy-two years of age now and living in New York City. Everyone close related to me is dead. Curly was executed against a wall by government soldiers in Bolivia way back in the day for trying to sell rifles to Che Guevara when the Cubans were there to cause a revolution. Darla took me to live in Argentina after that and then later to Florida, Orlando, to be exact, where I went to high school. I joined the air force and stayed in for twenty years, then became an air traffic controller at La Guardia airport and retired six years ago. I'm gay so New York is a good place for me to live. I don't know a thing about you except you grew up in New Orleans. I've visited there many times. As you must know it's a great city for gay people. Are you gay? My partner of fifteen years, Arthur Nub, who was a police officer in Brooklyn, died of prostate cancer a year ago. I have prostate cancer, too, but it's slow growing so I'll probably die of something else before it gets me. I hope you are free of disease.

"I would like to hear from you. I have two pensions and my social security so don't worry that I would be looking to borrow money. I'm just curious as you are the only living relative of mine that I know of. Are your parents still alive? My mama Darla died only six months back at the age of 100! She lived alone in Joplin, Missouri, and was killed when the roof of her house caved in on her when a big twister hit. She had a box of Mother Bizco Pancake Mix, her favorite, in her right hand and a frying pan in her left when they found her. Your cousin, Early Ripley"

Rain was falling steadily now. Pace put Early's letter on the desk and took off his jacket. He laughed a little, thinking about Early's life; about his father, Curly, being shot by a firing squad in Bolivia, and his hundred year old mother dying in a tornado with a frying pan in her hand. Early, a gay man living in New York, dying of prostate cancer, writing to a distant cousin he'd never met. There was nothing wrong with it, of course; this was life as it was lived and there was no need to try to make sense of it.

Pace remembered one thing he'd heard Sailor say about his cousin Curly. Pace had been about ten at the time and his father told Lula that when they were kids he and Curly once beat a water moccasin to death with tire tools, after which Curly bit into it, chewed a hunk of the snake's flesh and swallowed it. Lula asked Sailor why his cousin had done such a crazy thing, and Sailor said Curly said he'd heard if you ate a piece of a poisonous snake's body it would make you immune forever from snake bites. Pace wasn't sure if he would write back to Early or not, but if he did he would have to tell him that story.

The letter from Early reminded Pace of one of his most interesting childhood friends, Ignaz Rigó, who, following high school, had vanished into the greater world. Ignaz Rigó was a Gypsy kid whose family owned a two-story building on Barracks Street in the Lower Quarter. Pace had been to Ignaz's house a few times between the ages of thirteen and sixteen, and there never seemed to be fewer than twenty people, apparently all related, living there. The Rigó clan also occupied a storefront on Decatur Street, where the women, including Ignaz's mother and sisters, gave "psychic readings" and sold herbal remedies for a variety of complaints.

Ignaz, Senior, Pace's friend's father, called Popa, was always at the house on Barracks whenever Pace went there. Popa and an old man, Ignaz's maternal grandfather, named Grapellino, sat out on a second floor balcony on lawn chairs overlooking the street, talking and smoking. Both men were always wearing gray or brown Fedora hats, long-sleeved white shirts with gold cuff links buttoned at the neck, black trousers and brown sandals. Pace asked Ignaz what Popa's work was and Ignaz said that his father kept the family in order; and that Grapellino was a king in Vajra Dornei, which was in the old country. Pace asked Ignaz why, if his grandfather was a king in Vajra Dornei, he was living in New Orleans. Ignaz told Pace that Lupo Bobino, a bad king from Moldova, had poisoned Grapellino's first wife, Queen Nardis, and one of his daughters, and commanded a band of cutthroats that drove the Rigó clan out of Romania. Grapellino and Popa were planning to return soon to the old country to get their revenge and take back the kingdom stolen from them by Bobino's brigands.

"I'm goin' with them," Ignaz said. "We're gonna cut the throats of Lupo Bobino and everyone in his family, including the women and children. Last July, when I turned thirteen, Popa showed me the knife I'm gonna use. It once belonged to Suleiman the Magnificent, who ruled the Turks back when they kicked ass all over Asia. The handle's got precious jewels on it, rubies and emeralds, and the blade is made from the finest Spanish steel. Popa keeps it locked in a cabinet in his room. It's priceless."

Pace lost contact with Ignaz, who did not finish high

school with him. When Pace was twenty-one and back in N.O. on a visit from L.A., where he was then living, he went into the storefront on Decatur and asked one of Ignaz's older sisters, Arabella, who told fortunes and gave advice to women about how to please their husbands, where her brother was and what he was doing. Arabella, who was not married, had big brown eyes with dancing green flames in them, a hook nose, a mustache, and a thin, scraggly beard, as well as the largest hands Pace had ever seen on a woman. She told him that Ignaz was on a great journey, the destination of which she was forbidden to reveal. Arabella then offered Pace an herb called Night Tail she said would bring him good fortune with women, which he declined with thanks. Looking into Arabella's eyes, Pace remembered, made him feel weak, as did the thought of what she could do to him with her huge hands.

A year or so later, another former high school classmate of his, Enos Bidou, who worked for his father's house painting business in Slidell, told Pace that he'd run into Ignaz in Gulfport, Mississippi, where Ignaz was repairing roofs and paving driveways with his uncle, Repozo Rigó.

"Remember him?" Enos Bidou asked. Pace did not, so Enos said, "He went to jail when we were still at St. Tim the Impostor. Got clipped for sellin' fake Congo crocodile heads and phony Chinese panda paws."

"When we were thirteen or fourteen, Ignaz told me he would go one day to Romania or Moldova with his father and grandfather Grapellino to take back Grapellino's lost kingdom."

"Well, I seen him a month ago in Gulfport," Enos said. "He's got a beard now."

"So does his sister," said Pace.

6

Pace couldn't get Misty Tonga out of his mind. Her bold question regarding her attractiveness had made the intended effect on him and now Pace had to decide if he should make a serious move on her or let it pass. At his age, this took no small effort. He was twenty-four years older than Misty—what could she want, or expect, from him? Was she being merely casually flirtatious or did she genuinely desire Pace to pursue her? He disliked the uncertainty of it, this perilous game. She probably did not care, really, if she ever saw him again. And what was this Crusader Ralph nonsense, anyway? She was from a suburb of Los Angeles, an in-grown community of Pacific Islanders Pace had heard about when he lived in L.A. and worked in the movie business. Misty Tonga—her family was Tongan and she probably had seven or eight gigantic brothers.

The telephone rang.

"Hello?"

"Pace Ripley? This is Misty Tonga. Would you be agreeable to having a White Russian with me this afternoon?"

Pace woke up in a sweat. He had fallen asleep on the couch in the front room of the cottage. The phone call from Misty Tonga was only a dream. Pace was relieved but he felt ridiculous. He had read that dreams represented wishes and this possibility embarrassed him.

After rinsing his face, Pace stepped out his front door and took several deep breaths. The rain had stopped and the air was crisp and turning colder. What if Misty had invited him to join her for a drink? Would he have gone? Pace watched wet leaves being shoved along the ground by a sudden wind. He needed to get back to work on his book. There was no way to know how much time he had left to finish it. Misty Tonga could wait—and if she didn't, that would be all right, too.

7

Pace was never quite the same after he was shot. He recovered well enough to live much as he always had, but he knew something was missing, an inner strength or confidence that had been a reservoir of energy to defy whatever or whoever he felt was working against him. It was not a condition easily explained, not even to himself. Pace could handle this sign of vulnerability but it was not easy for him to get used to.

On the local radio station the morning after the day Pace dreamed that Misty Tonga called him, there was a bulletin alerting listeners to be on the lookout for a missing child, a seven year-old African-American girl from Bug Town, the community just west of Bay St. Clement, named Gagool Angola. Her mother, Oswaldina Capoverde, said that the child either had been kidnapped or run away, she didn't know which. Gagool's father, Rangoon "Ray-Ray" Angola, from whom Oswaldina was divorced, was doing a dime in Pee Dee for aggravated assault, so he was not a suspect if indeed the girl had been stolen. Gagool had been missing for forty-eight hours. She was described as being almond-skinned with a dime-sized, diamond-shaped birthmark below her left eye. When last seen she was wearing a white cotton dress decorated with red and yellow ladybugs, and her reddish-brown hair was tied in pigtails.

Pace stuck to his writing, concentrating on the period

immediately following Sailor's death in a car wreck, when Lula felt at loose ends, uncertain what to do with the rest of her life. It had been the most difficult time for Lula, more than those earlier stretches when Sailor was incarcerated. Her man's being gone forever was an altogether different situation; there was nobody to wait for, and Lula leaned heavily on Pace, as well as her best friend, Beany Thorn, for emotional support and sustenance.

It was late that afternoon, just past five o'clock, when Pace discovered Gagool Angola hiding in his woodshed. He had bent over to take an armload of small pieces for the stove and there she was, shivering in the white cotton dress spotted with ladybugs.

"Hey, girl," Pace said, "you lost?"

The child shook her head slowly from side to side, her eyes half-closed.

"Well, I can see you're cold. Come inside and get warm."

Pace gathered the wood he'd come for and motioned with his head for her to follow him, which she did, keeping back a few steps. Once they were in the cottage, Pace fed the fire in the wood stove and then draped a quilt around the girl's shoulders.

"Set yourself on the couch there, honey. Are you hungry?"

She nodded and said, "Thirsty, too."

"Okay, I'll make you a grilled cheese sandwich and hot chocolate. How does that sound? In the meantime, here's an apple."

Pace handed the apple to her. She grabbed it and took a big bite. One of her two front teeth was only half-descended. The diamond-shaped birthmark under her left eye was blue.

As Pace prepared the hot chocolate and grilled cheese sandwich, he asked the girl, "Is your name Gagool Angola?"

She finished the apple before answering, eating the core but not the stem, which she twisted and knotted around the pinky finger of her right hand.

"Um hum. I be name after a witch in a story my daddy know. How you know me?"

"I don't know you, but I heard on the radio that your mama is looking for you. She's afraid you might have been stolen."

Gagool laughed. It was not so much a laugh but a shriek, as if what Pace said was the funniest thing she'd ever heard.

"Nobody gon' steal me. I make too much trouble for 'em. That's why I run off. Mama say I'm too damn much trouble. I be too damn much trouble for you, too, you keep me."

"I won't keep you, Gagool. As soon as I finish up fixin' you this meal, I'm going to have to let the people who are searching for you know that you're here."

"I be gone before they come. I got no desire be finded."

"Come sit at the table," said Pace.

He set down a plate with the sandwich on it and a cup of hot chocolate. The girl shrugged the quilt off her shoulders, went over and sat down and took a bite out of the grilled cheese, then sipped the hot chocolate.

"Why don't you want to be found?"

"I'm big enough now to go see my daddy, so I'm goin'. He's in prison."

"Doesn't your mama sometimes take you to visit him?"

"Uh uh. She say he bad but he ain't, not even a little bit. Her new man, Bee Sting, be bad, and he don't like me. He hit me when he feel like it. My daddy never did. I tol' Bee Sting when my daddy Ray-Ray get out he gon' bust him up good and take me away."

"Your mama lets Bee Sting hit you?"

"She don't mind. She say I be doomded just like my daddy."

Pace knew he had to call the police but he stood and watched her eat. When she had finished the sandwich and drunk the hot chocolate, Pace asked Gagool if she was still hungry.

"Um hum. You got more?" she said, and smiled at him. He loved that her half front tooth stuck out the way it did.

"Comin' right up."

After he'd poured another cup of hot chocolate and made another sandwich, Pace went to his desk phone and dialed the police.

"I've got the little girl here you've been looking for. Gagool Angola, yes. The one from Bug Town. I found her hiding in my woodshed. She's fine, I've just given her something to eat. This is Pace Ripley. I live at the old Delahoussaye place off Rachel Road. But listen, she says she's been beaten by her mother's boyfriend, a guy called Bee Sting, so she ran away to visit her father who's serving time at Pee Dee. Okay, sure. Right."

Pace hung up. Gagool Angola was standing by the door.

"Thank you, mister," she said. "Now I'm goin'."

"No, honey, you've got to wait here for the people to fetch you. They'll make sure your mama's friend doesn't hit you again."

Gagool dashed out before Pace could stop her. He went after her but she had already disappeared in the darkness. Pace went back into the cottage to get a battery lantern and as soon as he had stepped outside again two police cruisers, their warning lights flashing, zoomed up the driveway. The cars stopped and four patrolmen got out.

"Where's the kid?" said one.

"She ran out of the house. I was just going to look for her."

"Spread out," the lead cop told the others, who split in three directions.

"Why didn't you lock her in?" he asked Pace.

"She was starving, so I fed her, then I called you. I didn't think she'd bolt like that."

The cop curled his upper lip and said, "I hate it when people think. You should have called us right away, before you fed her. Don't go anywhere."

He went to join his fellow officers in the search. Pace stood in front of his cottage. It was a moonless night. He figured the girl had headed for the woods behind Dalceda's house. Gagool, the evil witch, was a character in a novel by H. Rider Haggard, *King Solomon's Mines.* Pace had read it when he was fourteen. He wondered why anyone would name his daughter after her.

The world was a difficult place for a woman, Pace concluded. Punzy, lost and adrift, giving herself to Abstemio Cruz and worse; Bitsy, shot and killed by her humiliated husband; Misty Tonga, apparently under a spell cast electronically by a wigged-out ex-merc; poor little Gagool Angola, abused and driven from her home by some Neanderthal named Bee Sting; the list was endless, of course. He remembered John Lennon and Yoko Ono singing a song they'd written titled "Woman is the Nigger of the World." And then there were societies that forbade women education, didn't allow them to show their faces or exercise free will in any form, forced them to submit to cliterectomies, stoned them to death for looking at men other than their husbands. Neither were men spared victimization, or wild beasts slaughtered for food, baubles, clothing and medical research. This planet was certainly one wrong piece of work, which was no news at all.

After the police had left without finding the girl, Pace built up the fire in his wood stove and poured himself a triple shot of Glenmorangie. He took a hard swallow and thought some more about brave and hopefully not "doomded" Gagool Angola. She needed a chance to live her own life without being continually subjected to stupidity, cruelty and indifference. What could he do about it? Pace knocked back the rest of his Scotch and promised himself to find out.

8

Two days following his encounter with Gagool Angola, the police in Bay St. Clement telephoned Pace and asked him to come in and give an official account of what happened. The child had not yet been located but since Gagool had told Pace she was on her way to see her father, they expected her to show up at Pee Dee sooner or later. Pace complied with their request; it took him half an hour to recount the episode, and he made certain to suggest strongly that the authorities investigate this Bee Sting individual and not allow him to harm the girl should she be returned to the custody of her mother.

After he'd satisfied the cops, Pace noticed that it was five minutes past two, so he walked three blocks from the police station to Duguid's and went inside. Misty Tonga was not seated at the bar. Two heavyset, forty-ish men in overalls wearing Remington Ammo caps were drinking Rolling Rocks and loudly arguing about whether or not a particular call in a recent football game had been blown by an official. The same bartender as the other day was on duty. He nodded to Pace and came over to meet him at the end of the bar opposite the contentious pair.

"If you're lookin' for Princess White Russian, she ain't been in since you were here last. At least not on my shift."

Pace said, "Thanks," and turned to go.

"You sure you don't want a double Russki?" asked the bartender.

Pace waved his right hand from side to side over his head without looking back. He knew he had to check out the Crusader Ralph office, so he ambled down there. The sign was gone. He didn't bother to try the door this time. Driving home, Pace thought *Whatever Happened to Misty Tonga?* would be a good title for a mystery story.

He cut on the radio and was delighted to hear Sam the Sham and the Pharaohs sing: "Hey there, little Miss Riding Hood/ You sure are lookin' good/ You're everything a big, bad wolf could want." Pace remembered the first time he'd heard this song, while he was shooting pool one Friday afternoon in Johnny Reb's Roadhouse in Gonzalez, Louisiana, when he was eighteen. He and his high school buddies had gotten drunk, or close to it, that day on flat Dixie beer, and later ended up bruised and bloodied in a ditch after almost having had a bad accident on the highway in Flyboy Derondo's yellow 1954 Buick Roadmaster. When Sam the Sham and his bunch began howling like wolves, Pace joined in. As Beany Thorn used to say, sometimes all it takes is a little shoutin' to chase the devil off the porch.

Pace was in a good mood when he got out of his Pathfinder. The music had done its job. However, when he looked over at Dalceda's house and saw Gagool Angola sitting on the porch swing, Pace did not feel like shouting. He walked over and sat down next to the seven year-old girl.

"My legs is too short to make it go," she said.

Pace pushed off his heels and they swung. Gagool giggled, and just like her shriek, the sound was full of joy.

This time Pace decided to take the girl to Bay St. Clement himself, but only after cleaning her up a little and again feeding her a grilled cheese sandwich and hot chocolate, as she requested he do. Gagool did not resist being taken in but she made it plain that this was not her preference. She had been sleeping in a cemetery and did not know the direction to Pee Dee. A woman who lived across the street from the cemetery had seen Gagool wandering around and given her a bright red cloth coat with a rip in the back and a bag of stale doughnuts. The child told Pace that she had eluded capture by the cops after she'd run from his place by hiding at first in the woods where Pace had been shot. She asked Pace to please make the police promise to take her to visit Ray-Ray and he said he'd try.

Pace insisted on remaining at police headquarters until Gagool's mother arrived. Oswaldina Capoverde showed up accompanied by a large, bearded man wearing a lavender jump suit and a brown short-brim hat, whom Pace assumed was Bee Sting.

"You can't take her, Ms. Capoverde," the police captain told her. "There's been a complaint filed regarding the child's treatment and living conditions, so she'll be kept for the time being at the Child Services Center in Charlotte until a judge decides what's best for her. You'll be notified of the court date."

Oswaldina Capoverde demanded to see her daughter and yelled about how she knew what was best for Gagool, but she was not even allowed to see her. The large man grabbed Oswaldina by one arm and took her out before she made the situation worse. He did not say a word during the fifteen minutes or so that he and the woman were there, but he took note of Pace's interested presence and shot him an evil eye before leaving the station.

The matter was in the hands of Child Services now and there was nothing more Pace could do. He told the captain that Gagool wanted to see her father and the captain said that would be up to the authorities in Charlotte. They would be in contact with Pace in order to obtain a statement from him concerning the possibility of the child's having been abused, but because he was not related to Gagool he probably would not be allowed to be present at the hearing unless he filed a petition to be heard.

Outside a light snow was falling, an unusual event even in January in Bay St. Clement. Pace was glad that Gagool would not be sleeping in the cemetery that night. Oswaldina and her man were gone. Pace stood for a few moments on the front steps of the police station, allowing the snow to wet his hair, then he walked to the police parking lot and found that all four tires on his Pathfinder had been slashed.

9

To be a threat to somebody, all a person has to do is wake up in the morning. Did it really matter, Pace asked himself, if it was Bee Sting who slashed his tires? If so, Pace had to give him credit for so quickly detecting the correct vehicle to target, and for figuring out that Pace was the person who had filed a complaint concerning Bee Sting's behavior regarding Gagool. Of course, flattening—no, destroying—the tires was a warning, a dramatic message to cease interfering in a family matter. Replacing the tires had been an expensive nuisance. Pace had called Lula's old friend Oscarito at his service station, and his son—Oscarito, Jr.—had driven over with four new tires and changed them out. Pace appreciated Oscarito, Jr.'s quick work, especially in the falling snow, and tipped him handsomely.

As soon as he got home, Pace took out the Glenmorangie and finished off the bottle. He had to decide how deeply he wanted to become involved in the life of Gagool Angola. A solution that seemed feasible to him was to find a relative—a grandmother, or aunt, perhaps—who could, if willing, take responsibility for raising the girl. Pace certainly did not want to confront Bee Sting, or even Oswaldina Capoverde, but it could prove worthwhile to explore this possibility.

Pace had driven through Bug Town any number of times, but he did not know his way around the satellite community.

Snow had not accumulated on the ground, but the pothole-riddled streets were icy slick, so Pace drove cautiously the next morning, looking for a church. In a block of mostly ramshackle houses, he cruised slowly by a white wood building with the words BEYOND GOD AND THE DEVIL DISCIPLES OF LAZARUS on an unlit neon sign above the entrance. He stopped his Pathfinder, backed up, parked in front and got out. Flurries were flying now and a piercing wind caused Pace to narrow his shoulders and shiver in his thin leather coat as he walked on a broken sidewalk toward the front door. It was unlocked, so he opened it and entered.

The room was empty. Pace navigated his way through a disordered jumble of folding chairs and spotted a door off to one side. He went over and knocked on it. The door was opened by a tall, beautiful, beige-colored woman who looked to be in her early thirties. She had long, straight black hair and small grey eyes like scuffed pearls, and she was wearing a red sweatshirt with the word GIVE printed on the front; a large silver cross dangled on a chain hung around her neck. Her eyes met Pace's and she smiled, revealing several gold-plated teeth.

"We are those for whom Lazarus rose," she said. "Next service is at six."

"Pardon me for disturbing you," Pace said, "but my name is Pace Ripley and I've come to ask if you are acquainted with the family of Gagool Angola."

"Perfume James. I'm the pastor here. All of us in this community are at least aware of one another. What may I do for you?"

"I was wondering if you could tell me where I might find

relatives of this girl—grandparents, perhaps, aunts or uncles, cousins."

"Her mother lives on this street."

"It's not Gagool's mother I want to talk to. Are you familiar with recent events concerning the child?"

Perfume James studied Pace's face. They were the same height, six feet even.

"Would you mind explaining to me the purpose of your inquiry?"

"I'm the person who found Gagool after she went missing. Actually, she found me; twice, in fact. I was hoping that there might be a family member who could provide a safer and more stable environment for her than she's had until now. Gagool ran away for what I believe to be a good reason. She's a bright child in a dangerous situation, and I'm trying to be of help to her."

"We are all of us in danger, Mr.—Ripley, is it?"

Pace nodded.

"But I understand and sympathize with your concern. However, given the circumstances, despite your good intentions, I doubt that any attempt on your part to make an appeal on the child's behalf other than through professional channels would be appreciated. This is Bug Town, Mr. Ripley, and we are quite used to dealing with our own. With all due respect, my advice to you is to leave things be, lest you bring upon yourself unforeseen difficulties."

"I've already experienced one."

"All right, then. You're always welcome here. The Disciples of Lazarus are beyond God and the devil. We are risen for good reason, and, as you know, there are too many unenlightened souls wandering among us who are incapable of being reasonable. Be careful on your way out, the hall is a mess. Our congregation gets enthusiastic, if not downright unruly, sometimes. Coming back from the dead takes a great deal of effort."

She closed the door and Pace left the church. The man he assumed to be Bee Sting was seated behind the steering wheel of a dark green, cherried-out 1978 Mercury Monarch parked across the street, its engine idling. The bearded driver made sure Pace noticed him, viciously gunning the Monarch's motor, expelling acrid plumes of gray-brown smoke from his car's two sets of double exhaust pipes. After he was certain he'd gotten Pace's attention, the man drove ever so slowly forward and disappeared around the first corner.

Pace inspected all four of the Pathfinder's tires, satisfying himself that each of them was intact before he got in. Coming back from the dead, Perfume James said, takes great effort. Pace did not think he could do it, or even if, at this point, he would want to.

10

Pace never did hear from Child Services. Six weeks after he'd brought Gagool Angola to the Bay St. Clement police station, he called the station and asked to speak to the captain who had debriefed him. The captain was off duty and nobody else there knew anything about the case. Pace then called Child Services in Charlotte and asked a woman if she could tell him what determination had been made regarding the child. She asked Pace if he was related to Gagool. He said no, and began to explain his participation in the case, but the woman cut him off and said court decisions concerning juveniles were privileged information restricted to the family, and hung up.

It bothered Pace not knowing what happened to the girl. He thought about paying a visit to Perfume James, in the hope that the pastor could—or would—satisfy his curiosity; but then there would be the risk of running into Bee Sting, who seemed to be tuned in to his every move. Besides, Perfume James had advised him to let the situation play out without his becoming more involved. She was probably right, Pace thought. What happened to Gagool really was none of his business. It had been a fluke that she'd turned up at his place the first time, and the second time was due only to her not knowing where else to go. Moreover, he had not done Gagool any good, on both occasions having involved the police. Pace felt useless and dissatisfied, and could not shake the feeling.

He could, however, attend a service at Beyond God and the Devil, and not confront Perfume James directly. After all, she had told Pace that he was welcome, and so he drove over to Bug Town, arriving at the church a few minutes before six that evening. The chairs were properly aligned, all facing toward a small stage. Most were already occupied when Pace came in, and he took a seat at an end of the back row. He was the only white person among the twenty or so people in attendance, and all but two of the congregants, including Pace, were African-American women. Oswaldina Capoverde was not one of them.

At precisely six o'clock, Perfume James entered from the side room and climbed onto the stage. There was no pulpit and she carried no books or papers. She wore a plain white robe that covered her from neck to toe. Perfume surveyed the audience, seemingly inspecting each of their faces. She gave no special sign of recognition.

"'If the dead rise not,'" were her first words, "'then is Christ not raised.' After having been forced from the synagogue in Corinth, Paul took shelter in the house of Titus Justus, in close proximity to the temple, and continued to preach, though his assembly was small by comparison. We are alike, then, driven from accepted venues, and, as Lazarus, we are risen, sprung from darkness, freed from the cave where our eyes were bandaged, our hands and feet bound by those whose need engendered our subjugation. We who worship together now shall never again be manipulated into committing vile acts upon ourselves or others. We have seen the light and others see the light in us. Hallelujah!"

"Hallelujah!" the congregation responded.

The only man other than Pace among them stood up. He was old, in his eighties, perhaps even older, and he spoke in a trembling but audible voice.

"Pastor Perfume, the blessing of my blindness has enabled me to see. Can I get a witness?"

Shouts of "Amen!" and "Hallelujah!" issued forth from the gathering.

"My many years of drug addiction and the criminal life, even prison, were but instruction. Very soon I will be in that place Lazarus dwelt for four days before Jesus demanded the stone be rolled away. Shall I be risen thereupon to live a better life?"

"Pray, brother, as shall we, for the resurrection of your soul."

Again from the gathering came a chorus of approbation.

"When I dare to picture that child of fourteen on her knees in alleys and strange rooms, paid and beaten to pleasure men, in wonder I ask, 'Was that Perfume James?' And the answer I hear is 'No!' Perfume James has risen, she exists beyond God and the devil, as do all of you!"

There followed for the next two hours or more a spontaneous dialogue between the pastor and her devotees, after which each individual came forward and dropped a few bills or coins into a brass pot that had been placed at the foot of the stage. Perfume James remained standing next to the pot until everyone else, including Pace, had left the building. Outside on the sidewalk, Pace approached several of the women and asked if they had a moment to speak with him, but none of them would. He stood in front of the church and watched the congregants go, the blind octo- or nonagenarian being led away by a woman who appeared to be almost as old as he. It was very cold and Pace was about to leave when Perfume James stepped out and addressed him.

"Come back inside, Mr. Ripley, won't you?"

Pace turned and followed her. She closed the door behind him and sat down on a chair in the last row, as did he.

"When I was a child prostitute, one of the men who regularly availed himself of my services was Louis Delahoussaye. He was just another john, of course, but he was never violent or even verbally abusive to me. After his death, his widow found me and told me that Louis had left instructions for her to give me a certain amount of money if I were willing and proved able to change my life. Dalceda Delahoussaye helped me in this difficult endeavor, and it was her late husband's generous gift that enabled me to eventually purchase this building. This must seem a fantastic story to you, Mr. Ripley, especially that Mrs. Delahoussaye would accommodate Louis's wishes, but I assure you it's the truth, and I thought this would interest you."

"It most certainly does," said Pace. "It's an astonishing story."

"I thought to share this information with you in light of your interest in the child. I don't really know what will happen to her now that she has been returned to the custody of her mother, but she will have to find her own way, which is beyond God's way, and you must allow her to do so. The authorities have ordered that the man suspected of mistreating the girl not be allowed to live with them, and Child Services will be checking on the situation on a regular basis. I personally have visited the home and have offered to assist Oswaldina, even though she is not one of my parishioners, for the benefit of Gagool, in any manner that may be required. She seems amenable to my offer. So you may rest assured, Mr. Ripley, that some of us here in Bug Town are fulfilling our neighborly responsibilities."

Pace just stared at this lovely woman until she stood up and offered him her right hand. He stood and took it with his own.

"Have you ever been married?" Pace asked.

"No, have you?"

"Once, but briefly, a long time ago."

"Why do you ask?"

"Because you're the first woman I've ever met that I believe I could love completely and without reservation."

Perfume James flinched for a moment before she smiled and said, "Thank you for the thought, Mr. Ripley. You'd better go now."

Walking to his Pathfinder, Pace shuddered. He'd probably made a fool of himself, but he didn't care. He had spoken from his heart and he felt better for it. In *Proverbs*, he remembered, it says, "The man that wandereth out of the way of understanding shall remain in the congregation of the dead." It was good for him to know that he was still alive.

11

Pace wondered if Dalceda had ever told Marietta or Lula about Louis Delahoussaye's pedophiliac dalliances with and subsequent posthumous legacy to Perfume James, or if Dalceda had kept it a secret. If anything, she most likely would have shared this information with his grandmother. Marietta and Dalceda remained the closest of friends throughout their lives, just as his mother and Beany had. Dalceda undoubtedly needed to confide in someone, to unburden herself so as not to be eaten up by the worm in her brain that a terrible secret becomes.

The fantasy of his being able to have an intimate relationship with Perfume James persisted in Pace's mind. It was impossible, of course, and not only because he was close to being a half-century older than the pastor. There was her nightmarish past to consider, and now her religious calling. The idea was absurd, but much to his bewilderment Pace continued to agonize over it. He had become spellbound by this extraordinary woman, and he was in dire need of having the spell broken.

Pace stayed away from Bug Town. His links to both Gagool Angola and Perfume James were at best tenuous and pragmatically unrealistic. It was several days after his last visit to Perfume's church before Pace was able to resume working on his book. It was while he was writing one afternoon in the cottage when he heard the thunder of Bee Sting's Mercury Monarch disturb the silence. Leaving the motor running, the big man got out and stood in the driveway, holding an antique double-triggered 20 gauge Hinton shotgun with its twenty-seven inch Damascus barrels pointed directly at Pace's front door.

Pace looked out the window and froze, unsure of what to do. He waited and Bee Sting waited. After what seemed an eternity to Pace but was probably no more than two minutes, the big man put up the gun, spat on the ground, got back into his car and rumbled away. Pace sat at his desk, stunned. He was truly amazed that without any bad intentions on his part, his life could suddenly spin so dangerously and bizarrely out of control. Whenever he thought he was inching closer to the center of things, there appeared an intruder to deter or prevent him from moving any further. Perhaps the point was not to move but to remove himself.

"I'm surely in the way now, Daddy," Pace said aloud, "aren't I?"

12

Not that he probably needed added incentive, but just exactly what was the bug up Bee Sting's ass? The fact that Child Services ordered that he not share a household with Gagool and Oswaldina? Did he blame Pace for that? What else would inspire this thug to signify and threaten him? Having already been shotgunned once, Sailor Ripley's only son vowed to himself that he would not let it happen again. He cleaned and loaded his daddy's Colt Python and began carrying it with him whenever he left the property, kept it in the top drawer of his desk while he wrote, and on the floor next to his bed while he slept. Pace would have no compunction about taking the oafish Mr. Sting out of the count if need be. He would not initiate a confrontation but neither would he back away from it.

Pace was amused by this potential *High Noon* scenario. The image of himself at seventy years old, strapped and determined not to be intimidated by a Bug Town bully, carrying a ludicrous crush on a woman very much younger than himself, a former prostitute turned preacher, was a stretch of imagination Pace doubted even his former employer in the movie business, the director Phil Reál, who was renowned for his largely incomprehensible but darkly riveting films, such as *Mumblemouth* and the infamous *Cry of the Mute,* could feature.

Pace's dreams became increasingly confusing. In one, a gigantic spider seized the planet Earth in its eight sticky arms and began eating it, city after city, rotating the globe as he devoured entire countries, causing oceans and lakes and rivers to spill into outer space. In another, just as he was about to make love to a woman, she began to melt, her limbs and head dripping like candle wax until there was nothing for him to hold.

One afternoon, Pace drove to the ocean and sat in the Pathfinder looking at the water. It was a cold, windy day, and the beach below where he had parked was devoid of people. Then a black dog, a Labrador retriever, came trotting along by itself, dodging waves as he splashed ashore. Pace expected the dog's keeper to appear, but nobody did. The dog was making great sport timing his movements in order to barely avoid getting wet. That was it, Pace realized, his timing was off. He recalled his brief sojourn in Chicago, sitting on the back porch of his apartment late at night in all kinds of weather, listening to noises made by his neighbors, cats wailing in the alleys, dogs barking, gunshots in the distance. He had felt at peace there for a while both with the world and himself. That was more than ten years ago.

The black Lab finally tired of his game and ran off in the direction from which he had come. Could a dog discover the Up-Down? The wind picked up, buffeting the Pathfinder. Why not? Pace thought. A dog was a sentient being, just like he was. Pace took the Colt Python out of his coat pocket and laid it down on the passenger seat. A big gust of wind almost lifted the front end of the vehicle. Pace started it up, backed away, and headed for home. Just as he was about to turn off the beach road onto the two-lane to Bay St. Clement, the black dog dashed in front of the Pathfinder. Pace braked just in time to avoid hitting him.

"Thanks, buddy," Pace said. "Maybe I've got my timing back now."

13

Pace had not forgotten about the letter he received from his cousin, Early Ripley. However, the business with the little girl and then Perfume James had occupied most of his thoughts, to say nothing of the belligerent behavior on the part of his unintended adversary, the wolf ticket terrorist, Mr. Bee Sting. At this stage in his life, after the recent series of calamitous events, Pace was in no mood to make new friends. He did not want to appear impolite; nevertheless, Pace filed Early's letter in a bottom drawer of his desk. For some reason, Pace remembered being in the food line with Sailor at Rocky and Carlo's restaurant in Chalmette when he was about thirteen, and a refinery worker in his fifties, wearing his oil-stained uniform, standing in line behind them, said to his co-worker son, who was griping about something, "Eddie, I hate to admit it, but the best part of you ran down my leg."

It had been a long time since he'd been in New York, though, and Pace was curious to see how the city had changed since he and Rhoda had lived there. Given how unlikely it was that he could kindle a flame with the pastor, plus this stupid vendetta with his Bug Town stalker, Pace began to think about taking a break to revisit the big apple. A few days after he'd almost thrown away Early's letter, he retrieved it and dropped his cousin a note, saying he was pleased to hear from him, that he was planning a trip to New York, and suggesting that they get together. Early wrote back by return post: "Terrific! You can stay with me if you like. Tell me when you're coming." He included his phone number and e-mail address.

The morning Pace was packing a bag, preparing to drive to the Raleigh-Durham airport, Perfume James called him.

"Mr. Ripley, this is Pastor James. I hope I'm not disturbing you."

"No, of course not."

"I wanted to inform you that Gagool Angola shot and killed Bee Sting Goldberg last night. She's being held in detention at the Child Services facility in Charlotte. I'm going there today to see her and I thought perhaps you'd like to accompany me."

Pace hesitated before answering, trying to process this shocking development.

"Mr. Ripley? Are you still there?"

"Yes, yes. Certainly, I'll go with you. When do you want to leave?"

"Can you come now? I'd appreciate it if you could drive. Otherwise, I'll have to borrow a car or find someone else to take me."

"I'll be there as soon as I can."

"Pick me up at the church."

Pace hung up. Goldberg? Bee Sting's last name was Goldberg? He e-mailed Early Ripley that his trip had been delayed and that he would be in touch soon; then he cancelled his flight reservation. Before leaving the cottage, Pace put his revolver into the top drawer of his desk and locked it.

"Mama," he said, "you most probably won't be surprised to know that the world is still plenty weird on top, just as you left it."

The moment Pace's Pathfinder slid to a stop in front of Beyond God and the Devil Disciples of Lazarus, Perfume James came out, wearing a long, beaver coat with a hood, which she wore up over her head. A wet snow was blowing in.

"I saw you out the window," Perfume said, as she closed the passenger side door. "It's very kind of you to carry me over to Charlotte."

"I'm glad you called me. Can you tell me what happened?"

"All I know is that Bee Sting forced his way into the house and Oswaldina tried to get him to leave, which he wouldn't do. Apparently, he started beating on her and Gagool got hold of her mama's pistol and shot him in the back. Twice. Oswaldina called the police and told them that she had shot Bee Sting, but Gagool kept shouting, 'I done it! I done it!' Her prints were on the gun and they took the child away."

"He showed up at my place a week ago."

"Bee Sting did?"

"Got out of his Mercury with a shotgun and pointed it at my front door."

"Did he shoot?"

"No, just stood there, holding it. To warn me, I guess. I didn't go out, but he could see me staring at him through my window. After a bit, he drove away. I've been carrying a revolver ever since."

"You can't take it inside Child Services."

"I left it at home. I don't figure on needing a gun now that Bee Sting is gone. You said on the phone that his last name was Goldberg. How is that?"

"Mamie June Rivers, one of my parishioners, woman who gave me this fur coat, told me his father was a merchant seaman from Israel, met his mama in Baltimore, where Bee Sting grew up. According to Mamie June, his mama was on the game and his daddy disappeared. She took the man's last name, though, for Bee Sting, whose real first name was Abraham."

"Abe Goldberg."

"Uh huh. He made his livin' dealin' drugs over in Chapel Hill and Durham, sellin' to college kids. He got sweet on Oswaldina when she was workin' as an aide in a hospital somewhere there. They got together after he was in the emergency room bein' treated for a knife wound. Ever since, Bee Sting been Oswaldina's main man."

It was a two hour drive to Charlotte, but it went quickly for Pace, listening to Perfume James talk about her duties as pastor, how her former life of degradation and despair now seemed like somebody else's bad dream. She didn't ask Pace any questions about his own history, which he did not realize until after Perfume had been admitted to the visitors' room at Child Services. Having not received visiting permission in advance, Pace was made to wait in the lobby of the facility. Fortunately, he had anticipated this, and had put in his coat pocket a paperback copy of D.H. Lawrence's *Mornings in Mexico* that had been on his desk at the cottage. He was up to page thirty-nine, a passage that ends, "One wonders where he was, and what he was, in his sleep, he starts up so strange and wild and lost," when Perfume, whom he had not noticed re-enter the lobby, interrupted him.

"Thank you for your patience, Mr. Ripley."

Pace stood up and replaced *Mornings in Mexico* in his pocket.

"No problem, I had a book to read. How's the girl?"

"Come, I'll tell you in the car."

They walked out together. Once they were in the Pathfinder, Perfume James looked closely at Pace's face.

"You seem to have had a real effect on Gagool," she said.

"Me?"

"Yes. She told me that she wants to stay with you until her father gets out of prison. She says you made her good grilled cheese sandwiches."

Pace smiled. "I did. Twice."

"I told her that probably would not be possible, at least not for a while."

"What are they going to do with her?"

"Send her to a juvenile detention center for six months, maybe a year. After that, she'll go into foster care. I doubt that Oswaldina will ever be allowed to have custody of her daughter again. You could apply to be a foster parent."

Pace shook his head. "I'm too old. She'll need a good family, a father and a mother, other kids, to take care of her."

"I remember what you said to me at the church, about how you believed I was the first woman you could love completely and without reservation. Did you really mean it?"

"Yes, pastor, but I realized afterward how inappropriate it was, that I had doubtless offended you."

"You didn't offend me, quite the opposite. I was surprised, of course. That's a dangerous thing to tell a woman, any woman, but especially a whore who has found redemption."

Pace suddenly felt the cold. He started the engine and turned on the heater.

"Do you regret having said it?"

"No, I was sincere. I surprised myself."

"I can see I've embarrassed you, Mr. Ripley. I'm sorry."

"Can you call me Pace?"

She reached over and took both of his hands in hers.

"Yes, and when we're alone together, you call me Perfume."

Little pieces of ice were bouncing off of the windshield. Perfume tightened her grip on his hands.

"Pace," she said, "have you ever in your three score and ten had a woman with seven gold teeth?"

14

On Easter Sunday, a tornado tore through Bug Town and destroyed the Beyond God and the Devil building. Inside the church at the time were Pastor Perfume James and a dozen of her parishioners, early arrivals for the sacred day's service. As darkness descended and the unearthly howling increased, the thirteen women prayed for the twister to miss Bug Town and Bay St. Clement, believing as they did so that even if they were taken in the whirlwind, as Disciples of Lazarus they would rise again. The pastor and nine of the others gathered in a close circle in the center of the room died when the walls collapsed and the roof fell in on them.

Pace and Perfume had three good months together. He was in his cottage when the storm arrived. After he heard on the radio that the tornado had made a direct hit on Bug Town, he called the church but there was no response. When Perfume did not answer her cell phone, either, Pace could only hope that the Disciples of Lazarus would be justified in their faith.

During his time with Perfume James, Pace did not have much to do with her church. Perfume told Pace it was not necessary that he believe as she did, that it was enough if he had confidence in her ability to improve people's lives and inspire them to do the same. At Perfume's funeral, Pace spied Oswaldina on the fringe of mourners but did not speak to her. Mamie June Rivers, one of the three survivors of the church's destruction, was at the graveside. She told Pace that the pastor had spoken to her often of him and considered Pace to be further confirmation and living proof of her own salvation.

"I loved her," Pace said.

"We all did," said Mamie June Rivers. "Jesus, too. He'll return her to us one day, you'll see. They'll be walking side by side."

The day of the tornado had been Mamie June's eighty-seventh birthday. It was she who made sure that Perfume was buried wearing the beaver coat Mamie June had given her and which had become the pastor's favorite item of apparel.

A few months later, Pace prevailed upon the police captain in Bay St. Clement to find out for him what had become of Gagool Angola. The captain told Pace that Child Services informed him that the girl was living with a foster family in another part of the state. That was all he knew.

After Perfume James died, Pace stopped writing about Sailor and Lula. When he began again, after almost a year, Pace decided to tell his own story, to record the many unusual turns his life had taken, as well as his continuing search for the Up-Down. His objective, he realized, was not to make great literature—as if he could—or even be published, but to examine what he really thought had happened to him and those closest to him; and, if possible, to discover a few of the reasons why.

Pace recalled that In the gospel according to St. Matthew, the pastor's preferred witness in the New Testament, two blind men stopped Jesus as he was leaving Jericho on his way to Jerusalem, where he knew the Romans would torture and murder him.

"What can I do for you?" Jesus asked the blind men.

"If you are really the son of God and capable of performing miracles," one of the blind men said, "make us to see again."

Jesus passed one of his hands over both their faces, they opened their eyes and could see. The two men then joined Jesus and his disciples on their journey to Jerusalem.

Pace decided that from now on whenever people in need approached him, regardless of whether they appeared hostile or friendly, he would say only, "What can I do for you?" If he could help them, he would; if he could not, he would say so. What followed would be their responsibility.

Part Six

1

It wasn't just that getting old was no picnic, everyone knows that, but the thing that surprised Pace was how invisible one becomes. Throughout the first seventy-five years of his life—though he seriously doubted there would be a second seventy-five—Pace had maintained himself relatively well; he'd kept up his strength as best he could, and his mind, like Cool Hand Luke's, was right. He did not beg for company, entertaining himself mainly with his writing and reading. At seventy-seven, however, his eyesight had begun to fail; he also sustained a bad fall, breaking his left wrist when he lost his balance on the step-ladder while trying to reach a book on the top shelf of Louis Delahoussaye's library; and he had torn a muscle on the right side of his gluteus maximus stretching awkwardly to lift a stump he intended to chop up for firewood. As a younger man, Pace had been able to hoist a great deal of weight with one arm; he learned the hard way that those days would not come again.

He often thought about how different his life at this stage might have been had Pastor Perfume James not been killed a few years before in the infamous Easter tornado; that is, of course, if they had stayed together. Perfume was forty-two years younger and knew what she was getting into by hooking up with him, but she had insisted that the disparity in their ages did not matter to her, that with God's help she would deal with Pace's inevitable infirmities as they occurred. Perfume was certainly pleased that his cock came to attention in her presence without pharmaceutical assistance. Pace insisted that she take this as a compliment to her charms and she did.

It was easy for young folks to dismiss or ignore old people. The day before, on the street in Bay St. Clement, as Pace was coming out of Vincenzo's Plumbing Supply, where he had bought a new augur to snake a backed-up commode, a seven or eight year-old girl had come up to him and said, "You're ancient, mister." "Yes," he said, "I am." She reminded him of Gagool Angola, whom he had not seen in almost seven years. Gagool was now fourteen. She had probably forgotten Pace and most likely he would no longer recognize her. The thought of this stung him. Their few moments together, even during a difficult time, had been not merely memorable but sweet, even tender. It was enough, thought Pace, only because it had to be.

At the age of eighty, Lula, accompanied by her friend Beany, had embarked on what turned out to be her final road trip. Pace was not yet eighty, but he had not travelled in years and had the itch. He needed to go before his eyesight got any worse, or some unforeseen ailment seized his person. But where to? He'd not heard for five years from his cousin, Early Ripley, in New York, whom he had once planned to visit but never did. Early suffered from prostate cancer and was probably dead by now. Of course Pace could go to New York, anyway, but the idea did not appeal to him: too many people in too small a space.

He had been thinking lately about Mexico and Guatemala. The indigenous people there had understood the concept of the Up-Down, though that certainly had not tempered their proclivity for violent behavior. Visiting Uxmal, Chichen Itza and Tikal intrigued him. Pace had recently bought a used Toyota 4Runner with only forty-three thousand miles on it, after his ancient—like himself—Nissan Pathfinder had finally expired with just shy of three hundred thousand miles on her. The Toyota would work, but he needed a companion, not just someone to talk to, but in case one or more of his body parts failed him. Oscarito, Jr.'s son, Oscarito III, would be a good one. He was only thirty-two years old, unmarried, and a crack automobile mechanic, which skills could undoubtedly come in handy. Pace decided to ask Terry—short for Tercero, Spanish for third—as his daddy called him, if an all-expenses paid road trip to Old Mexico interested him. Of course Pace knew that it might be difficult for Terry to take time away from the service station and car repair business he and Oscarito, Jr., operated in Bay St. Clement, but it was worth a try.

To Pace's surprise and delight, Terry agreed to go. He told Pace, whom he had known for half of his life, that he could get away for two or three weeks at the beginning of December. "As long as we're back before Christmas," said Terry. "I can't miss my mama's birthday, which is Christmas Eve." Oscarito, Jr., thought it was a good idea, too, seeing as how his son had been working six or seven days a week for months.

Pace had more than a month to prepare for the trip, plenty of time to decide on a route and how much they might be able to accomplish over a relatively tight schedule. It would take too long to drive all the way to the Yucatan, let alone Guatemala, Pace figured, so he set his sights on their heading straight to Mexico City, where he'd never been, and seeing what happened once they got there.

"Plenty of sizzlin' little angels in Mexico City, I bet," Terry said.

"As the poet wrote," replied Pace, "We present ourselves among ignorant beasts by appearing as angels."

"Sounds good to me," said Terry.

2

Pace and Terry's trip proceeded uneventfully until they crossed the border into Mexico from Brownsville to Matamoros. It was in El Jabalí, a bar in Matamoros, that they met a man about Pace's age or older named Hugo Gresca, who spoke fluent English and told them he had worked for many years as an assistant to the movie director John Huston.

"I was the one who took Huston to Puerto Vallarta and found the location for him to shoot *Night of the Iguana*. He bought a property I discovered down the coast accessible only by boat. I was a young buck back then, a handsome devil, you'd better believe. Remember in that movie how Ava Gardner's always dancin' on the beach with those two caballeros shakin' maracas who're supposed to be her playthings? Well, scratch that, amigos. It was yours truly she took up with, taught me what she called the bullfighter's hello, which was to take her from behind when she didn't know you were there. She drank a lot and was losin' her looks a little, but she was a real woman. Those prancy-ass beach boys were maricones, both of 'em; they doted on Ava, though, brought her whatever she wanted: booze, boys, mota. She liked small men, married Mickey Rooney, for God's sake, and Sinatra, both shrimps. Ava lived in Madrid, mostly, at the Hotel Victoria, where the bullfighters stayed, and she had her pick. I got nothin' but good things to say about that woman.

"John took me to his estate in Ireland, where we drank whiskey every morning with breakfast, then chased foxes on horseback with the dogs. It rained all the time there and I needed the sun, so I went back to Puerto Vallarta and became the caretaker at John's hideaway for twenty years, off and on. It was a great life, amigos! Beyond dreams. After John died, I lived in New York for five years with Raquelita Pamposada, the Uruguayan actress known as La Pitonisa, the pythoness. She made only a few movies, most of them in Spain and Argentina, before she married a Swiss banker. The divorce settlement allowed her to live a life of luxury on Sutton Place, in a tri-level apartment above Katharine Hepburn's. This is where I met her, when John was spending time with Hepburn and Bogart before filming *The African Queen*. Raquelita had a very small part in that movie, as a Congolese prostitute Bogart's character consorts with prior to setting off on the river. She told me he had terribly bad breath and confessed to her that he could no longer get a hard on after too many years of hard drinking. Unfortunately, the Congolese whore part got cut out of the final version of the film because one of the producers thought it would prejudice the audience negatively toward Bogart. This was La Pitonisa's swan song, and nobody saw it. She showed me the reel and it was awful, though she was a knockout naked and painted black. I gave her the bullfighter's hello and goodbye both the first time I saw it.

"Later, the pythoness, who was famously lazy, grew quite fat and began spending her money and time at European spas, health farms, to lose weight. She had plastic surgery, too, which made her look like she was chewing tobacco all the time. Eventually, she preferred goin' to bed with women, gave up men, includin' me. Shot heroin, too, and sailed that Chinese junk straight to the isle of Lesbos. So, amigos, I made my slow exit, reluctantly, suffering humiliation upon humiliation. Despite her unsurpassed narcissism and diabolical behavior, I remained hopelessly in love with Raquelita. Only Dolores del Rio, or maybe Hedy Lamarr, had a face to rival the one she had before those witch doctors cut into it. Compared to La Pitonisa, Garbo might as well have been a chimpanzee."

Hugo Gresca's monologue, fueled by Cinco Estrellas and Negra Modelos, Pace and Terry realized, would not cease until he collapsed or died. They never did find out how Hugo had ended up in Matamoros because just as he started to tell them about a night he and Sean Connery and Huston spent in a Kabul whorehouse called The Den of Forbidden Fruit during the filming of *The Man Who Would Be King*, a very large, purple-black man wearing a crocodile-skin vest over his bare chest, entered the bar and lifted Gresca out of his chair and without saying a word carried him away.

Terry was awakened early the next morning in their motel by a call from his father. Terry's mother had had a heart attack and she was in the hospital. Pace drove Terry back across the border to a small airport in Brownsville, where he got on a plane to San Antonio. From there he could catch a flight to Raleigh-Durham or Charlotte. Pace again pointed his 4Runner south. He needed more of Mexico, or thought he did.

3

Pace drove on Highway 230 out of Matamoros to Monterrey and across the mountains to Saltillo, in the state of Coahuila. He had read about this part of the country, how in the middle of the 19th century, when the Austrian emperor Maximilian ruled Mexico, there had been a strong secessionist movement that resulted in battles between the insurrectionists and federal troops. It was during this period that the government of Coahuila granted sanctuary to the Black Seminoles, an integrated tribe from the United States comprised of Seminole Indians from Florida, breakaway Southern Creeks, who had fled relocation camps in Oklahoma, and fugitive slaves mostly from Texas. These people were called Mascogos by the Mexicans; they were unique in that they mixed freely and banded together against both slavehunters and the U.S. government. The Black Seminoles were allowed to settle in Coahuila in return for their help protecting villages along the U.S.-Mexico border from raiding Comanches and Apaches. The Mascogos became farmers and staunch supporters of the insurrectionists opposing Maximilian's army.

Pace stopped at the Hotel Río Salado, got a room, cleaned himself up a little, then went downstairs to the dining room. Only one other person was there, a tall, ruggedly handsome, broad-shouldered man in his forties, sitting at a table sipping through a straw what appeared to be fruit punch. As soon as this man saw Pace about to seat himself at another table, he stood up, motioned with a raised hand, and said, "Señor, if you would be so kind to join me."

Pace walked over and introduced himself, and the man said, "I am Aurelio Audaz."

They shook hands and sat down.

"As we are the only customers," said Aurelio Audaz, "I thought it could be agreeable to keep each other company."

"Por qué no?"

"Ah, you speak Spanish."

"Very little, I'm afraid. But your English is excellent."

"My mother was from San Francisco, California. At home we spoke English and Spanish interchangeably. May I ask what brings you to Saltillo?"

"I'm meandering toward Mexico City. I'm a tourist, never been to Mexico before. I live in North Carolina, though I grew up in New Orleans. And you?"

"I live in Coycacán, near Mexico City. I am here in Coahuila to hunt jaguars."

"Do the local cattle ranchers pay you for this service?"

"No, I do so for my own pleasure. I hunt exclusively with bow and arrow. Wild animals don't carry guns, so neither do I."

"They don't use bow and arrows, either."

"True, but the big cats are far more powerful and agile than human beings, and have large jaws with very sharp teeth that can crunch your bones, also razor-like claws that with a single swipe will remove a man's face."

"At least you're not going at it hand to paw."

"Not yet. I lie still and wait for the beast to come to me. It takes great patience."

A waiter came to their table. Pace ordered an Indio and accepted a menu from him. He went away.

"And when you are not tracking and lying in wait for jaguars, Señor Audaz?"

"I teach economics at a university in Mexico City. Hunting provides an agreeable contrast."

The waiter returned with Pace's beer.

"The *mole* here is excellent," said Aurelio Audaz. "I recommend it. They make it with chocolate."

"*Mole*, then," Pace told the waiter.

"Lo mismo para mí."

The waiter nodded and left.

"I've done some reading about the Black Seminoles," said Pace, "called Mascogos, who used to live in Coahuila. It's quite an interesting history."

"I know it. Their community was in Nacimiento. I encountered a descendant of the Mascogos once, twenty years ago in the foothills of the Sierra Madre Oriental. He was an old man, perhaps your age, but still sturdy. I was twenty-five. He challenged me to a knife fight."

"Why?"

Audaz shrugged his shoulders. "Quién sabe? Who knows? He was alone, as was I. Perhaps he was deranged, a mountain hermit. His clothes were torn, even his sombrero. He was dressed like a vaquero, but he had no horse. His skin was black yet his eyes were blue. You know there were whites among the Mascogos? They were not only Negro or Indian."

"William Powell was one," Pace said. "He was part white, one of their leaders from Florida. He renamed himself Osceola and led his tribe into the Everglades, where they took refuge."

"I would like to have met Osceola, the Seminole chief. He must have been a great warrior. He never surrendered to the United States government."

"That's right. The Seminoles refused to sign a treaty. Osceola was bayoneted to death at Fort Moultrie, in South Carolina. A doctor there decapitated the body and took Osceola's head to New York. It was destroyed in a fire."

"What a terrible indignity," said Aurelio Audaz.

The waiter arrived with two servings of *mole*.

"*Mole* was invented in Puebla," Audaz said. "Now you can get it almost anywhere in Mexico, but if you stop in Puebla, have it. They do it right."

Pace finished his beer and signaled to the waiter for another.

"Would you like a beer?" Pace asked Aurelio.

"No, gracias. I don't drink alcohol."

"You'll live longer."

"Maybe yes, maybe no. The most popular way for drunks to die is while driving."

"I'm sure it's best not to drink when hunting a jaguar."

"Fuera de duda, beyond any doubt. Unless, of course, the jaguar also has been drinking."

After they had finished eating, Pace suddenly felt weary.

"I'm sorry, Aurelio, but I must excuse myself now. I need to sleep. I'm an old man and driving a great distance tires me out."

Audaz stood up and extended his right hand.

"Of course, Señor Ripley. I leave before dawn tomorrow, so I'll say buen viaje to you now."

Pace shook his hand and said, "Good hunting to you, my friend. Don't let a big cat get his claws too close to your face. It's a good one."

"Muchas gracias. If it should happen, we would never meet again, and that would also be, if not a tragedy, a disappointment."

Pace turned to go, but then remembered Aurelio's story about his meeting the man in the mountains, and turned back.

"Tell me, Aurelio, what happened with you and the old Mascogo? Did you fight him?"

Audaz grinned and shook his head.

"No, he pulled out his knife, a very long, dark blade, stained from many years of use, from animal and perhaps men's blood, with uneven chips on the edge. I told him I was sure he had conquered many men braver than I, that I would be an insufficient test of his prowess. He stared hard at me for a long time, and at the moment when I became convinced he was going to lunge at me, seeing that he held his dagger with the cutting edge inward, so that his strokes be directed upward, as experienced knife fighters do, he returned his weapon to his belt and walked away."

"Good for you." said Pace.

"Sí," said Audaz, "but even better for him."

Pace slept well that night. A long-tailed animal with a tawny body and a black face appeared in a dream. When he woke up in the morning, Pace could not remember if it was a jaguar or not, only that it seemed to be pursuing a naked woman who was laughing as they both ran into darkness.

4

Late the following afternoon, Pace stopped at a roadside fruit stand to buy oranges and cherries. He stood next to his 4Runner and read the hand-painted sign: NARANJAS, MANZANAS, CEREZAS. Wind, dust, high clouds, beanfields. This felt and looked like what he expected Mexico to feel and look like. A short, portly, young woman wearing a brown dress with a thin, green rebozo around her shoulders, was stacking apples at the counter. A boy, about three years old, wearing only a faded red T-shirt, no pants or shoes, was pedaling a blue and white tricycle back and forth in front of the stand. Where were the flies? Pace expected flies but there were none; probably because the wind was blowing the stench of fertilizer or raw manure in the opposite direction. He was thinking about last night's dream: the jaguar, or puma, following the woman reminded him of Sailor, his lanky, loping gait; and the female had long, glistening black hair, like Lula's when she was young.

The little boy fell off his tricycle and started crying. The woman came around from behind the counter in a hurry, brushing against a small pile of apples, causing them to spill onto the ground. She was yelling, "Arriba, mijo! Arriba!" And she was laughing until two black Cadillac Escalades sped by with assault rifles firing from the rear passenger windows. The woman's face went dark and her shawl flew off as she ran toward the boy, shouting, "Abajo! Abajo!" before countless bullets tore into the fruit stand. Pace froze. He was still standing after the Cadillacs were gone. The boy was wailing, his tiny body covered by his mother's. She was not moving. Her last two words had been arriba and abajo, up and down.

Pace removed the boy and held him until he calmed down, then placed him in the front passenger seat of the 4Runner and buckled him in. Amazingly, his vehicle had not absorbed a single round. Pace found a few empty burlap sacks on the ground behind the counter of the fruit stand and used them, as well as her green rebozo, to cover the woman's body. He then drove himself and the boy back to Saltillo and took him into the Hotel Río Salado. Pace told the manager what had happened and he instructed two maids to take care of the boy. He asked Pace if he wanted him to notify the police.

"I've been told that in Mexico it's never a good idea to call the police," Pace said.

"The men who killed the woman must be narcotraficantes," said the manager, "drug runners, probably Los Zetas. They were shooting at the fruit stand for their amusement, and she got in the way. The police and los narcos have an accommodation. I will call the local authorities if you request it, but, unfortunately, I do not think the police will do anything other than to cause you delay, and, perhaps, to cost you money."

"What about the boy?"

"If he has family, we will find them. Do you wish to pass the night here, Señor Ripley? There would be no charges."

"No, gracias. Thank you for taking care of the boy."

Pace headed north. He would stay in Monterrey, then re-cross the border at Matamoros into Texas. There was nothing more for him now in Mexico. He turned on the radio and dialed in an American news station. The Vatican was considering the possibility of baptizing extraterrestrials.

5

The first call Pace made after he got home was to Terry and his father. Oscarito, Jr., answered the phone at his service station and told Pace that his wife was in stable condition and was expected to be able to leave the hospital in a few days. She was at Bay St. Clement Baptist but visitation was restricted to family members. Oscarito, Jr., thanked Pace for his concern and then passed the phone to his son, who wanted to know why Pace had come back so soon.

"Well, Terry, I ran into a situation just south of Saltillo that pretty much soured the trip for me. I'm all right, but there was an incident where a woman got murdered for no good reason and it literally turned me around. There are good people in Mexico but the country's kind of out of control, I guess. I'm not saying I won't go back there some time, just this isn't the time."

After assuring Terry that he would supply more details about the shooting when they were next together, and telling him how glad he was that his mother was recovering well, Pace rang off. He sat at the kitchen table in his cottage, drinking peppermint tea. It was almost noon and frost was still on the ground. Three blackbirds were pecking at something in the grass next to the driveway in front of Dalceda's house. Pace recalled an old saying from his childhood: If you see blackbirds on the ground in January, it will snow. There were a few days left in December, so perhaps, he thought, snow will fall sooner.

The fact that the young woman who died at the fruit stand protecting her little boy shouted in Spanish the words for up and down could not have been a coincidence. Or could it? Had it been a sign, or a warning? Did the episode have any meaning regarding his search for the Up-Down? Pace was in a quandary. Perhaps it was foolish to attach significance to such a horrendous event, which had nothing to do with his being there. But why had he not been shot, too? Bullets were whizzing everywhere: How could they all have missed him? Pace realized that he was crying. Tears from his eyes were falling into the teacup.

He stood up and walked outside. The blackbirds ignored him, continuing their pecking at what Pace could now see were the remains of an opossum. He had not cried since Perfume James's funeral. He was still in shock, he realized, from the incident in Mexico. When in danger, Pace remembered, possums often feign death, in the hope that their pursuers or adversaries will lose interest and leave them alone. When the shooting at the fruit stand started, Pace had not had time to even think about playing dead; yet, unreasonable as he knew it was, he felt guilty that he was alive and the woman was dead. At least her child had survived.

It was too cold outside to cry. Two of the blackbirds took off; the one that remained strutted around the carcass a couple of times before pulling at the possum's tail. Pace went back inside the cottage. He decided to write a letter to the family of the woman who died, to tell them how heroic she was, that her selfless, final act saved her son's life. He would mail it to the manager of the Hotel Río Salado and ask him to please see that it was delivered into the proper hands. Pace thought it was important that the boy know of his mother's bravery and her sacrifice. He regretted that he could not write the letter in Spanish.

That night, Pace dreamt again of the jaguar and the woman, only this time, after the pair had been running for a while, the woman turned to look back at the bounding feline but he was no longer there. She stopped running, and Pace woke up. He looked out the window. It was not yet dawn and snow was falling.

6

It was unseasonably warm the morning of Pace's 80th birthday. This was July weather, not October's. Marnie Kowalski had called at six a.m. from New Orleans to wish him a happy birthday. She was sixty-four and already up and baking; in fact, she told Pace, she was about to open a second bakery, in Uptown, near Tulane, called Magdalena's, in honor of her mother, whose cake and pie recipes were the foundation of Kowalski Cake & Pie Company in the French Quarter.

Pace was on his second cup of coffee, reading a revised translation of Proust's *La Prisonnière*, and was in mid-passage wherein Morel is being excoriated for his detestable behavior, when the sound of tires crunching gravel in his driveway forced him to stop. An old Ford pick-up truck parked between the house and the cottage, and a tall, slender, teenaged girl got out of the passenger side.

"This is it, Daddy!" she shouted.

A well-built black man of average height came around from the driver's side and stood beside the girl. Their mutual resemblance was unmistakable. Pace went out to greet them.

As soon as the girl saw Pace, she smiled and said, "Mister, do you remember me? I'm Gagool Angola, and this is my daddy."

Pace walked over to her, nodded his head, and said, "I most certainly do, Gagool. You're all grown up now."

"I'm seventeen."

The man came forward and extended a hand.

"I'm Rangoon Angola."

"Ray-Ray," said Pace, and shook hands. "My name is Pace Ripley."

"Gagool has told me many times how kind you were to her when she run off."

"He made me grilled cheese sandwiches and hot chocolate."

"I been in a correctional institution, sir, been out now six months, and she be after me to find this place and thank you for your help in her difficult time."

"I didn't really help your daughter so much, Mr. Angola. I did feed her, though."

"A couple times," said Gagool.

"Would you like to come inside?"

"No, thank you. We're on our way to Atlanta."

Pace looked over at the old pick-up.

"You sure that truck will make it to Atlanta?"

"Drives better than it looks. I got a job waitin' on me there."

"Daddy's a minister in the First Ethiopian Church of the Queen of Sheba. He's gonna preach and I'm gonna sing in the Daughters of Zion choir. I'm a good singer, good as Beyoncé. After I finish high school in Atlanta, I'm goin' to New York or Hollywood, get on a talent show, make records and perform all over the world."

"I hope you do, Gagool. As I recall, Ray-Ray, you were up at Pee Dee."

"Yes, sir, for ten years."

"My daddy did time there, too."

Rangoon Angola shook his head and said, "It's a painful

place to be. If it ain't been for me findin' the path taken by the Queen of Sheba followin' her hook-up with King Solomon, I might still be lost in the desert."

"Daddy's a Son of Sheba."

"Sheba had a son by Solomon," said Ray-Ray, "therefore, we who spread the words she heard from Solomon are also sons."

"Probably better these days to be in Atlanta than in Ethiopia."

"The founder of First Ethiopian, the Reverend Doctor Mandrake Ammanadib, handed down my instructions when I was a captive. My destiny is written, as is yours."

"Mr. Ripley," Gagool said, stepping toward him, "do you mind if I give you a hug?"

"Of course not."

She embraced Pace and kissed him on the top of his head. Gagool was now taller than he was.

"Thank you, Gagool. Today is my birthday, and I couldn't imagine receiving a better gift than seeing you happy and reunited with your father."

She pointed over at the porch on Dalceda's house and said, "Remember when we sat on the swing and my legs were too short to make it go, so you did it?"

Pace laughed and nodded.

"That was the last time I was happy for a long time," she said.

Rangoon Angola and Pace shook hands again.

"I'm glad you've found your way," Pace said to him.

"We all of us hold swords," said the soon-to-be minister of the First Ethiopian Church of the Queen of Sheba in Atlanta, Georgia.

As Gagool and her father drove away, it occurred to Pace that Ray-Ray had referred to himself when he'd been in Pee Dee as a captive, which, of course, was the title in English of the story of Proust's that he had been reading when they arrived. Pace was reminded of a confusing movie he had seen many years before, *Orpheus Looks Back*, in which a detective investigating a murder says to his partner, "There's no such thing as a bad coincidence."

A bluebird landed a few feet away and looked at him.

"I guess this is as good a day as any to be eighty years old," Pace said. "Isn't it, Daddy?"

7

Often when Pace reflected upon his life, he thought that nothing of real significance had happened; at least insofar as his actions were concerned. Not that he had not gone out into the world and looked around, he had, and come into contact with all kinds of people, both good and bad. But had anything profound occurred by the fact of his having existed? Who but himself could even consider the gravity of such a question? He was convinced that in terms of merit he had fallen short; the world could have easily gotten along without him, as it soon would, anyway. Surrounded as he had been by so many people who ostensibly were invested in an ontological belief system, he never could buy a word of any of it. He did, however, finally understand that the Up-Down was the house he lived in, and always had. Why had nobody ever told him? When he spoke to Sailor or Lula, he expected them to answer, he really did. So what if they were dead? That woman who died during a tornado holding a frying pan in her hand; the young mother gunned down at the fruit stand; Perfume James when the roof fell in; Dr. Furbo with a hypodermic needle in his ankle; Rhoda Gombowicz dismembered by men, not the gorillas she chose to live among. What was intelligent about such a design? The Shoshone knew: We are all of us trapped in the Up-Down. Perhaps I did die when I fell off a cliff in Wyoming, Pace thought, or when the hunter in the orange hat shot me through the back and the heart; maybe that's why I was unharmed by the barrage of bullets in Mexico, because I was already dead, and only now am I beginning to accept it.

Part Seven

Pace still wrote occasionally. Having long since completed his book about Sailor and Lula, he added now and then to his memoir. It was odd, though, how the ways in which he remembered individuals varied greatly depending on his mood of the moment. At times these characters seemed to him larger than life, so colorful and exciting they must have existed only in his wildest imagination. Other times, these same people appeared in a dimmer light: sad or pathetic rather than exuberant or heroic. The magic of memory was undependable, erratic at best. Age certainly had something to do with it. Now an octogenarian, Pace remained stubborn in his pursuit of accuracy in depicting persons he had known. The world would continue to change but the dead could not; therefore, if any of them were to be remembered and written about, it was imperative that he resist the temptations to either mythologize or unfairly disparage.

Pace was fortunate that his health was good enough to enable him to continue living independently. His eyesight had not deteriorated appreciably since a measurable decline three or four years before. He could read in daylight without glasses; it was his night vision that suffered, so he avoided driving after dark whenever possible. Tercero, as he preferred to be called now, was a great help to Pace maintaining the Delahoussaye property; and Tercero's wife of two years,

Angelina, came out from Bay St. Clement three evenings a week to prepare Pace's dinner and make sure he had the necessary household goods and toiletries. Pace complained that Tercero and Angelina were overdoing it, but in truth he enjoyed the attention and their company.

He never had gotten back to Mexico, nor had he heard from Gagool Angola since her brief visit with her father en route to Atlanta. Pace occasionally checked out television shows such as *American Idol* and their ilk in the hope that Gagool would appear, but either he had missed her or she was still singing exclusively with the Daughters of Zion. Marnie Kowalski called every week or two, just to make certain Pace was above ground, as she liked to say, never failing to remind him how fond of him she was and always would be. A day did not pass that he did not think of Perfume James; their lightning-like liaison had burned a mark on him impossible to ignore or erase, not that he wished to do so. Pace likened it to one of his favorite old horror movies, *Mark of the Vampire*, with Bela Lugosi. Perfume had bitten into his soul, she was in his blood, so part of her would always be with him.

When the small grays arrived, Pace was not surprised. It was in late August and the air was warm even at three o'clock in the morning. He had not heard their spacecraft land, but he assumed it was in a clearing in the woods on the other side of Dalceda's house. Several of the visitors were gathered outside between the house and the cottage. Pace observed them through his bedroom window. The grays were each about five feet tall. They did not have mouths but Pace heard them talking, making squealing sounds, regularly gesturing with their extremely long arms and three-fingered hands.

Their two eyes were very large, covering a third of their faces, but never blinking; they had no eyelids. There were two holes on either side of their heads, which Pace guessed were auditory components. No visible genitals; wide, partially-webbed feet; protruding bellies; smooth, unwrinkled rumps.

The squealing conversations continued for the better part of an hour. Pace was not sure exactly how long the grays were there because he fell back to sleep, and when he woke up at six-thirty, they were gone. Pace dressed and walked over to the clearing. There was a deep, circular impression in the ground, and many branches of the surrounding trees had broken off. The only other evidence of the aliens' presence that Pace could find were a few semi-webbed footprints in the dirt next to the steps leading up to Dalceda's house.

Pace camped out on the porch of the house for the following five nights, hoping that the grays would return, but they did not. He remained confident they would, though, and hoped he would be there when they did. Pace did not tell Tercero or Angelina about the spaceship landing, and did not bring to anyone's attention the signs in the clearing; nor did he write about the event. If Sailor had been alive, Pace would have told him. His daddy would have camped out on the porch, too.

2

Pace remembered that in her letter to him following Lula's death, Dalceda Delahoussaye confessed that she had never really believed in God or the devil—who she dismissed as "an excuse exists in stupid peoples' minds"—or in the Big Bang Theory, either. Pace was on a similar wavelength. He did not discount entirely the physicists' explanation that the universe was a result of a big bang, but who or what lit the fuse? There was still a long way to go, he figured, toward explaining the set-up for this explosion. He would ask the small grays what they knew about it, if he got the chance.

"Disney against the metaphysicals," Ezra Pound wrote in the last of his *Cantos*. Truth in fantasy versus falseness in science. It was useless to expect a definitive answer, so why do people try so hard to sell one? For money and power, of course. Those were temporary rewards but for some—perhaps most—they were enough. True believers were better off for providing a fix for their own insecurities; and *The Road to Enlightenment* should have been the title of a final Bob Hope and Bing Crosby movie.

Pace was in a cynical mood. He rose from the kitchen table and went outside to chop kindling. He looked up and there was the constellation of Cassiopeia, queen of Ethiopia. Perseus had arrived there holding the head of Medusa, the Gorgon, whom he had slain. Did Rangoon Angola know that story? If Gagool were here, Pace would tell her about Perseus and Andromeda and Cassiopeia, who, according to the poet Milton, was black, like her, and was so beautiful that after her death she was placed among the stars. Had Gagool become a star yet?

Pace cut into a block of wood with his hatchet. Among all of the people he had known, there were only a few Pace truly missed, and Gagool Angola was one. He would see her again, if it was in the stars.

3

During his earliest years, when Sailor was in prison in Huntsville, doing ten years for his part in an attempted armed robbery of a feed store in Big Tuna, Texas, that resulted in the maiming of an employee and the death of Sailor's accomplice, Bobby Peru, Pace was raised exclusively by his mother, with occasional assistance from his grandmama Marietta. Lula never visited Sailor while he was incarcerated but regularly corresponded with him, providing details of Pace's development. She remained faithful to Sailor, rarely even entertaining the thought of being with another man. Lula explained to Pace that his daddy had made a bad mistake by allowing himself to be coerced into committing a serious crime. Lula was pregnant with Pace at the time, and she and Sailor were out of money, stranded in West Texas. Sailor's foolish act was born out of desperation, and he was fortunate not to have been cut down along with the black angel Bobby Peru. He promised Lula that he never again would betray her trust in him, and in all of their years together following his release, he had not.

Pace did not really miss his daddy while Sailor was in the penitentiary due to the circumstance of his never having known him. Lula worked during those years at odd jobs, mostly waitressing, in New Orleans, and accepted supplementary financial help from Marietta, who doted on her only grandchild and refused to allow him to suffer for want of proper clothes or food or decent housing because of poor decisions made by her daughter and Pace's lunkhead daddy. Lula was an attentive mother and always put her son's needs above her own. She retained her spirit of independence and feisty character, however, which frequently sparked conflicts between Marietta and herself, but her mother recognized and acknowledged Lula's devotion to Pace, and so maintained civil relations with her, but from a distance. Marietta's fervent desire that Lula end her relations with Sailor Ripley did not, of course, come to pass, a situation that Marietta eventually came to terms with, albeit reluctantly. True love was a condition Marietta Fortune had not experienced, therefore it was difficult, if not impossible, for her to fully appreciate the concept. Prior to her death, however, having witnessed Sailor's turnaround and well-intentioned parenting of Pace, she told Lula that Sailor had gained her respect, an unexpected gesture that satisfied her daughter and enabled Lula to think more generously about Marietta in the years following her mother's passing.

Lula's fidelity to Sailor faced a severe test only once, when Pace was seven and a half years old. Lula was not working at the time she met a trumpet player named Duke Davis one night when she and a dancer friend of hers named Baby Doll DuQuoin were having a nightcap in Renaldo's Martini, a club on Iberville Street. Baby Doll—she swore that was her real Christian name—had danced in a show in Miami that Duke's band had played in a year or so before they met up at Renaldo's Martini. Duke was thirty-five years old, from Chicago, where he lived with his wife and three children, as

Baby Doll was quick to inform Lula. Davis was not very tall but dark and handsome, with impeccable manners, and Lula could not help but be attracted to him. As she later admitted to Beany Thorn, he reminded her of Sailor, the way he moved and gestured with his hands, even his voice. Duke was in N.O. working a weeklong gig at the DeSalvo Hotel. He had a drink with the two women and exchanged small talk with Baby Doll, who gave him her phone number and told him to call if he had time. After ten minutes, Duke excused himself—the band had a final set to play at one a.m.—and left, but not before paying for their drinks.

"Seems like a nice guy," Lula said.

"I would have gone to bed with him in Miami," said Baby Doll, "but one of the other girls, Lorna Dune, who's a porn actress now, got him away from me. I couldn't compete with her 36-double D's. She sat on his lap, let her top drop, and put one tit in each of his hands. Skinny little me was toast."

At noon the next day, Duke Davis called Lula.

"How did you get my number?" she asked him.

"From Baby Doll. I'm free until nine tonight. Would you like to have lunch with me? How about Galatoire's, at three?"

Without hesitating, Lula said yes. Duke said, "Great!" and hung up. She was more than a little surprised at herself for capitulating so quickly, and considered calling Duke back, but she didn't have his number or know where he was staying. She decided to stand him up, but after she picked up Pace from school at three-fifteen, she drove down to the Quarter, parked her car, and entered Galatoire's at a quarter to four with Pace in tow.

Duke Davis was sitting at a table against the far wall,

drinking a Bloody Mary. As soon as he spotted Lula, he stood up and waved, smiling broadly. Then he noticed Pace, lost his smile a bit, but put it back before they reached his table.

"I thought perhaps you'd found something better to do," Duke said.

"Had to fetch my son from school. Pace, this is Duke. Duke, this is Pace."

Duke took the boy's small hand in his own big one and said, "Glad to know you, son."

"What's wrong with your lip?" Pace asked. "You get punched?"

Duke grinned and Lula said, "Mr. Davis is a trumpet player, Pace. If you play it for a long time, the mouthpiece leaves an impression."

"It's called an embouchure, son. That's the way a musician applies his lips and tongue to a wind instrument."

"I'm Sailor Ripley's son, mister, not yours. He's in prison in Texas. You gonna have that embutcher forever? It's ugly."

"Why don't we all sit down?" said Duke.

Pace never forgot having lunch that day at Galatoire's. Duke Davis kept trying to hold his mother's hands and she kept pulling them away. Afterwards, when they were standing on Bourbon Street in front of the restaurant, Duke Davis asked Pace if he'd like to take a ride in a carriage pulled by a mule, and Pace said, "You take it, we got a car."

Lula met Duke by herself in the bar of the DeSalvo between sets the evening before he and his band left for Chicago. He had phoned her several times after their luncheon date, wanting her to meet him following his gig, but she told him that was too late, that she had to be up early to take Pace to school.

When she said she had to go, Duke walked Lula outside and around the corner into Père Ferdinand Alley, where he gently but firmly pushed her up against a wall, kissed her and put his right hand under her skirt between her legs. Lula let him keep it there while they kissed, then pushed him away.

"You're wet," said Duke.

"Your wife's pussy probably is, too," she said. "Have a good trip to Chicago."

The next day, Baby Doll called Lula and asked how her date with Duke had gone.

"It wasn't a date, Baby Doll. We just had a drink before his band went on again."

"You didn't stay?"

"No, I went home."

"Shoot, Lula, I wanted to know what his dick is like."

"You should have asked Lorna Dune."

Pace did not know that his mother had seen Duke Davis again following their lunch at Galatoire's. One day three years later, after Sailor and Lula were reunited, while the three of them were watching Louis Armstrong play cornet and sing on a television show, Sailor said, "I wonder how it feels for a woman to kiss a man with a split lip like Satchmo's."

"It's called an embutcher," said Pace.

4

The morning was cloudy and cold with a whiff of moisture in the air. Pace had been awake since four-thirty; rarely these days did he sleep more than four or five hours at a stretch. The time now was twenty past seven. For the last hour or so he had been reading Wilfred Thesiger's fascinating book, *Arabian Sands*, a personal account of the British explorer's crossing of the Empty Quarter of Arabia from 1945 to 1950, before oil was discovered in the region and changed forever the vast expanse of desert then occupied almost exclusively by Bedouins. Thesiger had spent most of his adult life among the Arabs, only in his penultimate years residing in Kenya; and then, in his final, fading days, back in England, where he died at the age of ninety-three. The Oxford-educated Thesiger had led a daring existence, experiencing deprivation of various kinds and danger during his travels, distinguishing himself by his service in World War II, and capturing it all brilliantly in his books. Pace did not expect to live to be ninety-three, but that was only ten years from now, so it was a possibility. After all, what was the alternative? He still felt pretty good on most days, and to his knowledge no antagonistic termites were gnawing on his insides.

Pace had been deeply impressed by the scene in the film *Lawrence of Arabia* where Lawrence is seized by the notion of approaching Aqaba by land, crossing an expanse of desert known by the Bedu as The Devil's Anvil. The Turkish guns in Aqaba face the sea; therefore, he reasons, Prince Faisal's army, with whom the British are allied, could blind side the enemy. To carry out this audacious enterprise, Lawrence takes fifty men, who, against all odds, cross the forbidden Nafud desert, then—aided by a rogue Arab tribe—attack the Turks from the rear and conquer Aqaba. Thesiger was a chance-taker in this mold, possibly the last of his kind. Pace would have liked to have been an explorer with a purpose: like Lawrence, fighting to unite the Arabs; or Thesiger, mapping previously uncharted territory. Unfortunately for him, this was not to be—not written, as the Arabs say. Even acts of ingenuity and bravery unravel given time and political chicanery. T.E. Lawrence was betrayed by his government and by himself; Thesiger was put out of business by the ways of the world. Life itself was a cautionary tale, and Pace's difficult conclusion was that he had lived his too cautiously. Men such as Lawrence and Thesiger had a measure of greatness in them; by what stick, Pace wondered, would his life be measured?

After having had his coffee, blueberry muffin and a banana, Pace went for a walk in the woods; as always, since the almost-fatal shooting mishap of several years before, keeping an eye out for rogue hunters. He did not, however, expect to encounter a dozen young Chinese women bound together by a thick, tight rope in the middle of the clearing where the spaceship bearing the small grays had landed. The women were wearing only thin black jackets and pants; they were crying and shivering, having apparently spent the previous night exposed to the elements. All of them looked to be in their teens or early twenties. When they saw Pace approaching, they began talking loudly to him all at once in Mandarin.

"Please, I don't understand Chinese," he told them, gesturing as he came closer with his arms extended, trying to calm them down. "Do any of you speak English?"

"Yes," said one. "We slave girl, come bottom ship. Men put in truck, make stay until come back."

Pace took out his pocket knife and cut the rope strand by strand as he spoke to her.

"What is your name?"

"Li. Man bring Ah Kung. Buy girl China family. All afraid."

"Do you know where Ah Kung is taking you?"

"Work city. New York."

Pace had almost severed the rope and was trying to decide what to do about the women when he heard a tractor-trailer truck drive up and come to a stop on the dirt road at the eastern side of the woods that bordered the field. Two men, one Chinese, one white, entered the clearing on foot. The white man was carrying a rifle. The women's wailing increased. Pace continued cutting the rope as the two men advanced toward the group.

"What're you doin' here?" the white man shouted at him.

"I own this land. You're trespassing."

"Just comin' to pick up our property," the man said, "then we'll be on our way. Best you leave off workin' on that rope."

Pace cut through the last strand and stood up straight, facing the men. He folded his pocket knife and put it in his coat pocket. The Chinese man began barking at the women. They all stood up.

"He Ah Kung," Li told Pace. "Say he own, must go him."

The snakehead was a small man dressed in a blue suit and white shirt without a tie, wearing a New York Mets baseball cap. It was hard to tell how old he was. Pace guessed forty. The man with the rifle was big, more than six feet tall, two hundred and fifty pounds, with a thick reddish-brown beard. He had on a long, black leather coat and a floppy leather hat.

"These women are illegals, aren't they?" Pace said.

"Ain't none of your business, mister," said the bearded man. "Get on your way and so will we and that'll be the end of it."

"They're on my land, so I'm responsible for them now. You two can go, but I'll take care of your cargo."

Ah Kung started shouting louder and was shoving the women, motioning for them to walk toward the path through the woods by which he and the other man had entered the clearing.

"The hell you will," the big man said to Pace, and pointed his rifle at Pace's chest.

The snakehead struck Li across the face and twisted one of her arms. There was nothing Pace could do to prevent the two smugglers from herding the women toward their truck without risking his own safety. He half-expected the big guy to shoot him anyway. Pace watched them all march away, but walked quickly in the same direction after Ah Kung and his accomplice disappeared into the thicket. He kept out of sight until the women had been loaded into the container and the men had boarded the cab of the truck, then crept closer, took out a pen and small wire notebook from his coat pocket, and copied down the license number on the truck as well as the code letters and model number on the container.

Pace hurried back to his cottage, called the Highway Patrol

and gave the information to an officer. He had done the only thing he reasonably could do. Li and the other women were no doubt intended to be forced into prostitution or to work in sweat shops in New York's Chinatown. Pace searched the internet for news of female trafficking from China, hoping to find out something about Ah Kung that might be of help to the FBI or INS. The only mention of a man by that name was an article from the *San Francisco Chronicle* newspaper, dated September 23, 1912:

> Chinatown was stirred into uneasiness last night by the news, quickly learned by every Chinese, that a secret meeting of representatives of the tongs engaged in slave girl traffic had been held and that a price of $2000 had been set upon the head of the man who is believed to have betrayed the presence of three slave girls rescued from 5 St. Louis Alley a few days ago by Sergeant Arthur Layne and Captain Frank Ainsworth of the Immigration Bureau. As a result Sergeant Layne at Central Station dispatched a detail of uniformed men into the alleys to assist the Chinatown Squad. The spectacular raid by Layne which resulted in the capture of Ah Kung, in addition to the three slave girls, valued at $3500 each, was the culmination of a number of similar rescues, each of which, rumor has it, resulted from betrayal by Chinese "stool pigeons." The tong men have sought to discover the informer and the action of offering $2000 for certain

identification is expected to cause trouble. That the presence of three slave girls was betrayed to Captain Ainsworth first, instead of to the police, caused suspicion to fall on Loy Yee, proprietor of a disorderly house at 7 St. Louis Alley, running in competition to the one raided. Loy Yee quickly took cover after protesting his innocence to Ray Gatchalian of the Chinatown Squad.

Pace never did hear back from the Highway Patrol or read anything about the Chinese women hidden in his woods. Was it possible that this Ah Kung could be a descendant of the Ah Kung arrested in San Francisco for slave girl trafficking more than a century ago? Pace was dazed by this latest bizarre experience. First the gathering of small grays, and now a dozen Chinese slave girls, all of them aliens. Strange, he thought, how that same word was used to designate human beings from his own planet as well as extraterrestrials; and both had by some crazy coincidence appeared within days in the same small clearing in the woods behind his house in North Carolina.

"Mama," he said, "this is more than weird. I sure do hope I get the chance to tell you about it."

5

Pace's dreams consumed him. Lula appeared in most of them, usually as her older self and often in need of his help, which in reality was almost never the case. His mother remained mobile and able to care for herself until the end of her life. Others who were featured, in various contexts, were Rhoda, Marnie, Perfume James, Gagool, the devilish Rattler brothers, who were killed when Pace was a teenager, Phil Reál, Beany Thorn, his grandmama Marietta, and, of course, Sailor.

The situations involved family gatherings, reunions with old friends and adversaries, and occasional encounters with unrecognizable people, all relatively benign. The worst dreams were those in which Pace was by himself in an airport or train station in a foreign country and had lost his ticket or passport; he was stranded without money or identification, in the midst of a fast-moving crowd of travellers speaking languages unknown to him.

Pace thought these dreams foretold what awaited him after death, both the good and the bad, neither heaven nor hell; only a kind of restless netherworld, not the sanctuary he desired. It did not matter what a person had done during his or her lifetime, Pace decided, whether they had helped or hindered or hurt others; death, also, would pass.

◎   ◎   ◎

It was Angelina who found Pace's body lying on the ground next to the woodpile. She had brought a freshly killed chicken, broccoli and chocolate ice cream for his Thursday dinner. After Angelina phoned Tercero and gave him la dolorosa, as he called it, the bad news, she put the groceries into the refrigerator in the cottage, made a pot of coffee, and sat down at the kitchen table to wait for her husband.

Six days later, a letter arrived for Pace that was never opened and not returned to sender by the post office in Bay St. Clement for lack of a return address.

Dear Mister Pace Ripley,

I dearly hope this letter gets to you even though I don't have your proper address. I figure the p.o. in Bay St. Clement will know and deliver it. I never have forgot your tenderness to me when I was a runaway little girl you never saw before. That girl is now in Los Angeles. No she is not a famous singer or movie star. Not yet! She is working as a hostess in a restaurant in Santa Monica and taking singing and dancing and acting lessons. Her daddy is in Atlanta but he had a stroke last year and can't preach any more. He still goes to the First Ethiopian Church of the Queen of Sheba and sits and listens and prays. Mostly for his daughter he says. The people there take good care of him and she calls him every Saturday morning. Ray-Ray puts you in his prayers too. His daughter is sure he would like you to know that. Mr. Ripley I am all right but I do get sad a lot. I don't know if my mama is alive or the drugs got her. I get nightmares sometimes about what I done to Bee Sting. It's very hard for me to get really close to anybody a boy or a girl. You probably understand this problem because you are so smart. I hope this will change some day. I want you to know you are always in my own prayers right at the top along with Daddy. If you ever pray pray for me too okay. One more thing I don't use the name Gagool out here it was too strange. Now my name is Cassie short for Cassiopeia who was a black queen of Ethiopia like Sheba. There is a star named after her.

Cassie (Gagool) Angola

CODA

Pace Ripley's writings were found by Angelina when she was packing up his possessions. She gave them to Tercero, who contacted Marnie Kowalski, in the hope she would know what to do with them. Marnie asked Tercero to please send the manuscripts to her in New Orleans, which he did. In his will, Pace had left the Delahoussaye property to Tercero and Angelina, which was a complete surprise to them; a most welcome one since she was pregnant and they were soon to be in need of more ample living quarters.

Marnie read every word Pace had written: both the 2,500 pages about the lives of Sailor and Lula, and his 1,700 page memoir recorded in the form of a diary. She showed the Sailor and Lula manuscript to one of her regular customers at Magdalena's who was a professor in the English department at Tulane University. He read and recommended it to a publisher he knew in New York, who liked it and edited Pace's enormous novel and published it. Very few people bought the book, but Marnie was thrilled, just as she knew Pace would have been. She sincerely believed there were people out there in the world who would discover and be as profoundly moved by it as she was. After all, it was a genuine true-love story, and there could never be too many of those. Pace's memoir Marnie kept to herself; it was too personal, she felt, for anyone who had not known him intimately to read. The diary was his truth, and the truth is always best kept to one's self.

ABOUT THE AUTHOR

Barry Gifford's fiction, non-fiction and poetry have been published in twenty-eight languages. His novel *Night People* was awarded the Premio Brancati, established by Pier Paolo Pasolini and Alberto Moravia, in Italy, and he has been the recipient of awards from PEN, the National Endowment for the Arts, the American Library Association, the Writers Guild of America, and the Christopher Isherwood Foundation. His books *Sailor's Holiday* and *The Phantom Father* were each named a Notable Book of the Year by the *New York Times*, and his book *Wyoming* was named a Novel of the Year by the *Los Angeles Times*. He has written librettos for operas by the composers Toru Takemitsu, Ichiro Nodaira and Olga Neuwirth. Gifford's work has appeared in many publications, including *The New Yorker*, *Punch*, *Esquire*, *La Nouvelle Revue Française*, *El País*, *La Repubblica*, *Rolling Stone*, *Brick*, *Film Comment*, *El Universal*, *Projections*, and the *New York Times*. His film credits include *Wild at Heart*, *Perdita Durango*, *Lost Highway*, *City of Ghosts*, *Ball Lightning*, and *The Phantom Father*. Barry Gifford's most recent books are *Sailor & Lula: The Complete Novels*, *Sad Stories of the Death of Kings*, *Imagining Paradise: New & Selected Poems* and *The Roy Stories*. He lives in the San Francisco Bay Area. For more information visit www.BarryGifford.com.